72

To Henry &

THE
EXPERIENTIAL FEAR

Almut

Best Regards

+ V R H

GW00502506

northern lights

Tony.

Some of the stories in this collection have appeared in different form and under different titles in the following publications: The Record, edition of the Transport and General Workers (1979-1981), The Seaman's Charter (1982), History Workshop Journal (1978, 1986, 1988), Roughshod Magazine (1975), North West Labour History Journal (1990), and International Big Issue (1993).

Published by Northern Lights
P. O. Box 302
Liverpool
L69 8JQ

First published 1996

Copyright © Tony Wailey 1996.
The moral rights of the author have been asserted

ISBN: 0 9527624 0 4

This book is sold subject to the condition that it shall not, by way of trade or otherwise, be lent, re-sold, hired out, or otherwise circulated without the publishers prior consent in any form of binding or cover other than that in which it is published and without a similar condition including this condition being imposed on the subsequent purchaser.

Designed and typeset by SoftNet Ltd, London
Printed and bound by The Book Factory, London

By the same author

Living the Fishing.

The Balance of Strange Times.

Other Countries Have Their History.

for Patrick Cavan

There is that which helps you believe
in something else besides death:
somebody in a car approaching
on a street too narrow,
and he or she pulls aside to let you
by, or the old fighter Beau Jack
shining shoes
after blowing the entire bankroll
on parties
on women
on parasites,
humming, breathing on the leather,
working the rag
looking up and saying:
"What the hell, I had it for a
while. That beats the other"

Charles Bukowski, "One for the shoeshine man."

CONTENTS

INTRODUCTION

By nearly all standards, but particularly those of literature, these stories are failures. They have been around too long and have picked up too many reject letters. Most of them say, "the material is good, the fiction is awkward." So these are awkward stories about awkward people and the supreme failure lies in that awkwardness which nevertheless struggles to have its experience validated but lacks the art to complete the picture.

Nowadays however it is possible to get academic credit for a certain kind of non recognition. It is called "experiential learning". In other words what had previously kept you out of an institution - be it a university or anything else that goes by that name - is now what can get you in.The records of previously ordained failure show that what you learned from your experiences can now add up to something more than you imagined.

This ought to suit some of us quite well. The Institution takes us in, we can question what we like, stumble upon enlightenment, then return to some outer darkness with some finer phrases, some sadder songs, some more beautiful flowers to string across the chains as Marx would put it or later, C Wright Mills.

These stories come from the displacement of the working class. And what better basis might there be in these blown out years of reaction than the experience of the Celtic fringe within the British working class. And how better to articulate its long slow fracturing than with the clumsy sensitivity sought in these pages. The worn cardigan or the sharp suit has many pockets, each loaded with its own little quota of cultural capital to set against the more or less empty wallet, except for the photographs, that has served us all, just enough, for so long after the post-war "golden age". Now, even the angels in marble are only a month away from dispossession.

The world of the steelworks or the mines and the shipyard

always had a tighter frame on which to stretch its community than the paradoxical and contradictory world of the waterfront with its intense localism and far horizons. In Liverpool, my home city, this world has almost gone, to be replaced with the more desperate casual labour of half a century before, with little of the strength that fed the city from the river. Only the angry humour remains. But if there is no reason for nostalgia we still need to record the experience of that disconnection.

In similar fashion the stories have their own fractured existence. My own experiences as seaman, construction worker, student, researcher, teacher and adviser with adult learners serve what some sociologists would call "spliced lives". But as we go along, making the same mistakes, we learn, poco a poco, to weigh these bits of cultural capital differently. Differently, in that we cannot tell in advance what knowledge we will make our own. The tension between home and flight, community and self, rootedness and metropolitan glitz remains and recurs. And still we believe, all of us, that our experience will be assessed, credited and somehow validated, however unlikely.

That same fracturing is evident in the range of experiences people are bringing forward to present their past lives for assessment and recognition. Experiential Learning helps to provide us with some sense of what is happening in the realisation that the process is not simply a rational one and though a collection of experiences are much more indirect to formal learning than we would like them to be, what can be learned from that displacement is common to us all. This is the reason why these stories are offered in return, not only for vanity and status but rather as other versions of the ones heard every day in our Advice Centre from either the third world, the inner city, the perimeter estates or the outer suburbs. From the culture of work to the culture of learning to the culture of what passes for culture itself we are trying to spell out what this might mean in the current cycle of dispossession.

We live in power or powerlessness. The successful author of fiction has the power to create an illusion. The voices of the

8

powerless have their own illusion of truth. These stories attempt to connect the two just as Higher Education now, with its high sounding, often empty rhetoric flirts with the desires and fears for itself and its new entrants. There should be nothing to fear, of course, as Old Gorky knew, eighty years ago, when he described the teeming wharves of Odessa as, "my universities", before he spent time in Sorrento and Capri, creating other illusions.

These stories are then rich in failure, the failure of time to deliver, the failure of talent, the failure of hope - who would ever publish them - but they also illustrate, the hopes and dreams that pass daily in and out of the revolving doors of the new universities. They grasp for recognition just as the hundred hands stretch for the ball when it is kicked into the crowd, the great cocktails of learning imprinted on every palm, the demand to be heard, to bear witness if only to say, "Well fuck you anyway," as they wait for the next great trap or sudden enlightenment.

THE LIVERPOOL BEACH

'It's ten past three' rings down the bar
Through Bootle and Dingle and where else the scar
Cuts through dreams of juke box listeners
Seeking ships without a whisper,
Hearing all the sea within you.

The telephones have hushed on Burma,
Rantung, Kantash, Tierra Fuega.
No ship's rating steams out of China,
The Yankee Bar is just a reminder.
Listen to the sea still thunder.

No Malabar Booker nor Pacific Steam
Pulls its lode line to Belem,
Nor takes cargo east of Chaqua
Through the Chanos to Antofogasta.
The sea still rolls and sways beneath you.

No roaring sighs of Yokahama,
No more duck boats with bananas.
The not too cool of modern poetry
Hits Spanish streets from the 'Velarde'.
In the corner the quiet man singing,
No rebel roar as once sang Geordie.
Land of the dawn with every signal
Blows no more through San Francisco
Do not dance the sad fandango
Listen to the sea inside you.

Does it still remind you when
You propped the bars of trip and turn.
Teeming outcast hopes are sweetened
Change the record like the seasons
What is one from life around you?
Last nights shore in the market diner,
Taking cargo to Rhode Island
No soldiers then in Valparaiso
Just singing swinging dancing gusto.
Don't give up on that inside you.

Remember Billy at Pernambuco
Squirming through to broach the cargo
Whispering below the slats 'It's goodo',
All for big strides in Chicago
Listen to that sea inside you.

That battered roll that swollen sea
Those 'barefoot days' of every party.
Awash with drink and flyblown visions
And midnight dancing beats decisions
Let it swish and roar inside you.

Anchored off the coast Tampico
Night time sailing through white Islands
Garbled cry of warm tequila
Tasting sweeter from the stealing
Drunken silence deep within you.

Still on Sunday at Puerto Ocampo
Green sea rolling Mar Del Plato
No docks and slaughterhouse Buenos Aires
All is quiet on the 'Olivares'
Pastel is the sunlit cabin.
And then on down to Punta Arena
No Brooklyn Bridge no Santa Juanita
Just Macquarrie, Newcastle, Sydney
You're going down again to Aussie
Going down the fool within you
And coming home with gay bravado
Two years later where did that go?
Try to dam the introspection
The river quiet the docks reflection
All the roaring sewn within you.

Remember the poet's imperial line
From black and swollen slaving times
'My name is Bordeaux and Nantes and Liverpool,
New York and San Francisco,
Not a corner of this world but
Carries my thumb print and dirt'.
From docks that held the sail then diesel
With quayside high and ships with names on.
Now look down the sunlit Mersey
No marker lights that bloodstained history.

Let's get fucken' back to Malacca
Find some huwers east of Java
What the shite are we doing here.
Drowning drip by drop in fear
Where the fuck have all the years gone.

Gone in ships you fool sin numero
Play the jukebox to remind you
First the old song then the growing
fear like the time is blowing
For the union and the seamen.

And the hell were you in 'sixty?
Shouts the old lad across the jukey
and 'forty seven and 'twenty five
When we needed bread to live
Where the shite were you all then?

Billy, Billy catch yourself
The Mersey is this dockland bar
Where every bastard comes with scars
There never was much fucken here
And what is left is not worth having.
Atlantic boxes and drifts of timber
and colossal weights without a docker
Humped and shifted all in silence
Where once the job paid church attendance
A card a shilling a union button
Now the toiling all forgotten
Three on the hook three on the dole
Even the good times down the hole
Buck up Billy and dance the Samba
But the Liverpool river is gone forever.

The Liverpool River, the Celtic Sea
Land of shithouses and bad poetry
Hurtled from our jiggered homes
Millions of us went to roam
On ships that rode and stalked these waters.

It's ten past three Bill mind your way,
Mind your way when clocks are broken
And wonder which clubs are open
For all those ships, this weeks giro
The sea still thunders to remind you.

Go on home Bill it's well gone time
Mind your way when bells have rang
The landlords music, where else is open
To hear those ships and lives who've spoken
Listen to them sound inside you.

Go on home Bill find your way now
Find your way when every sinew
Strives to make the hours continue
With every fucken port you've been to
And the sea still crashes deep within you.

BRING IT ALL HOME

He felt the weight of the telegram in his pocket. He felt it crumble as if his insides had been knotted, he sat there still. He knew the words well enough. The language was simple in the way the in-laws spoke.

"Father passed away today, funeral on Wednesday."

The sound of the train was a slow clatter of wheels on rail as they made their way North towards the border. Late in the winter afternoon, the city train station seemed far far away, and clouds slate blue and garlanded with red hung low over the Meseta. Inside the carriages the light seeped. It seemed strange that the drizzle and bustle of Barcelona, the mass of colour highlighted in the rain that poured around the brownstone colonnades and squares and made trees weep and crowds bow to traffic, should all have passed as quickly as the day; as if in the time they had taken to deliver.

They had given it to him in the bar when the postman could not find his address. The message was a day late and he cursed for the sweat to be home in time; then all he could think about was the train and the rushing North. "Malas Noticias, bad news?" the grey haired old owner had asked.

"My old man is dead." said Jackie, almost unaware, his mind full of thought.

The lad sitting opposite him gave a shudder and turned his face away as if to hide from the station where porters were stacking fruit. Turned as if from the City itself, with its hot perfumes and reeking drains.

"This place" he shuddered in disgust and shook his head.

Jackie looked at him. He looked to be going home as well.

By this time the train was passing through the industrial villages and suburbs. These were the new buildings and new houses of outer Barcelona, clustered together amidst piles of newly laid drainage schemes. Floating streets, the colour of brown mud, and great puddles of greasy yellow light glistened in the rain. People stood in groups under the alcove of a long bar and watched the train go by. Many of them looked

16

pale from shift work and with the black stubble outlining their features, their faces had a curious haunted look, as if something vital had been forced away from them.

"See those people" the lad waved an arm, "they're waiting for something. Sometimes they wait all their lives and they die, kicking and struggling because what they have been waiting for hasn't yet happened. They watch every passing train and they think of relatives who have gone and they wonder" He shrugged, "I haven't time to wonder any more."

The rest of the journey passed by in silence and Jackie drank from the bottle as the carriage clattered forward in the gathering dark, and thought of Mexico where he might have been heading.

"Passed away." The wording was as smooth as stone and dignified in a quiet sort of way, and he would not know until later that he'd collapsed in the toilet and the fire brigade had to hack the door down before his body could be brought out, and how the old lady had sat alone through the ashes of the night.

The train rocked on the tracks, swinging her way inland until the lights of the Meseta fell behind them and from village squares shadows crossed over waiting faces. The frontier was spreading before them like a jeweller laying out his wares, and France appeared, the pearls of Europe in the folds of her black border.

The immigrants stood huddled in pockets of twos and threes. The threadbare remains of some forgotten army waiting forlornly on the platform, waiting for the train to take them, to despatch them from that desolate patch as the night grew longer and colder; to anywhere. The black coats were thin and shiny with wear, and the inhabitants faces were held down into the folds as they huddled together and tried to escape the wind. They would not have seen the stars out high over the platform nor the terraces and silent shapes of the Pyrenees.

The host country offered little communion, the few

houses built of stone; hung wooden shutters kept out any warm glow that might be offered the itinerants, and all there was by way of comfort was a man trying to sell sandwiches and lukewarm coffee. A stained white overall was pulled across his coat and his voice sang out in the cold; it looked for all the world like some play from biblical times, but no one wanted to give a performance out here. A procession of lost souls, a platform awash with hope, take your choice. The vagrants set off from here to all parts of Europe.

As the train came up out of the sidings, the younger ones amongst them tried to laugh and make jokes, but most were quiet and turned their faces out of the wind, and ran anxious eyes over the bundles of belongings they were soon to haul aboard. Their faces shone clearly under the lights, some of their women were with them and some of the children but it was hard to tell who looked the saddest, those with their families or those going alone.

You could sense a stale emptiness in the air, the unmistakeable smell of travel and fatigue that hung like a cloud as they were ushered along the platform beyond the customs hut to the train. One or two shouted to keep their spirits up and were told by the uniformed customs to keep quiet. They were in France now.

And France bolted past the carriage window all that night. There were another five in the compartment with Jackie and all had wine and all shared it around. In the corner were two gypsy lads from Andalusia whose family had moved to Barcelona, but not far enough for them. Two dark good looking lads who kept talking and clapping their hands as if to scare away their thoughts. One of them turned to Jack and said, " If we work hard and learn the language and try the ways of the French, we'll be all right."

Across from them a welder from Valencia gave a grunt and said, " You can walk and talk like a prince, but they'll still treat you like shit."

The boy's face coloured in anger and he turned away, but the welder was holding the bottle towards him, "It's the same with this" he said, "You have to find out for yourself." He had lived in Paris before, had all his papers and a job waiting, and still he knew the horrors of that city. These two had nothing and they thought they were walking into something big. He sat back in his seat when the bottle came round again, his bald head shining in the railway light.

Two girls were sat in the carriage. One of them, with a child's face and nervous continuous laugh, was going to England and another, a dark, stout girl from Navarre who hardly said a word during the first hours, was on her way to Paris and nodded her thanks to the welder as he passed over the drink. The wine was emptied in laughter and a few songs as the moon rose high in the sky and the French plain went by in a blur. Jackie was slowly drunk, and like others overladen with care and suddenly released, rooted deeper in his bags for more booze that might be hidden. And with his fellow companions emerged with bundles of fruit and cognac, tins of sardines, dry biscuits and crusts of cheese, anything to keep the fanfare going. And as each became loosened with the drink, the enormity of their future lives loomed large and was spoken about in low murmurs, that were just as suddenly drowned in song. The welder talked of renting a small flat after six months and maybe having enough to bring his family to France. The gypsy said he would walk his feet off rather than return home a failure. His brother and the nervous little girl were slowly falling to sleep, and the girl from Navarre had closed her eyes but you had the feeling she was listening to it all.

In the carriage itself, it seemed as if a space between the travellers had been bathed with an unreal finish of muted light, diminished by reality like one of those old brown photographs taken from the past; above them the racks were stuffed with luggage and pictures of the Marne shook with vibration on the wall, the rear of the train and the blur of its passage in the night seemed to have a life all its own, and against this backcloth were strewn the sleeping faces suddenly unveiled, as if at a wake when the lights were turned low and a blue lamp used to guard the darkness.

Sleep was difficult for Jackie so he lay there, head back in the twilight, and it was from there with his head on the rest and the roar of the train through the tunnels, that the welder as a shape moved across the dark girl and began to kiss and fondle her. She made no movement and he fondled her slowly and his hand moved up her legs and deliberately stopped and he whispered then carried on until slowly she undid the buttons of her slacks and eased them down over her thighs . The white flesh showed above her stockings as she eased herself down the seat the welders hand within the fabric of her underclothes until with their arms around each other they lay down on the carriage floor and Jackie felt the warm outpouring of their breath as it panted into the night.

He came awake with an early light stealing like silver across the fields. The girl from Navarre was back in her seat and smoked as she looked out of the window. The Welder slept deeply, slumped, his head resting on a bundle of clothing. His hand was behind the girls back, as if it had fallen from her shoulder. When Jackie opened his eyes she said good morning and smiled.

The carriage smelled of sweat and stale smoke and last nights drink and even tho' it was cold, they opened the windows to freshen the place. Paris was no more than an hour away. The realisation was beginning to hit home. The train journey was an illusion, an escape, yet here was the reality no further than a few miles. Nobody spoke, yet all began to shift in their seats and watch deliberately as the small towns gave way to the Parisian suburbia, as if somehow preparing them for the advent of the big city.

The engine pulled them into the Austerlitz. Beyond it, the colossus that fed on petrol fumes and concrete and spawned from the depths of the warm and comfortable suburbs, battered their presence with its roar, larger than any train. Travellers were caught and exposed to its madness, to the frenetic blur of its traffic, to the coldness of the inmates, workers in the blackened glass spires they call offices who had been spewed into daylight by their metro, and shuffled with their secretaries in marionettes of colour along the pavement.

Cars honked and bleated and roared as cascades rippled down the streets and the smell of coffee and wine hung like smoke in the air. Paris with its people, the smells, the very strangeness, bit like a sudden pain across the faces of the travellers; lonely emigres standing on the platform of the big station hugging their scant belongings to themselves as if they were crown jewels beneath the cold November sky.

There was nothing left to say, that was the terrible thing this morning. Who hadn't laughed or drunk or sung when the night was like a lifetime away; now in the cold morning a terrible emptiness was everywhere. The welder and the dark girl kissed each other and even walked part of the way to the station entrance before they went different ways. The gypsies shook Jackies hand and said they would never be failures. Suddenly desolate, he took their hands as if their offerings could help him forget. The gaunt iron spars of the station roof turned him giddy and buffeted by the shouts of the baggage men as they scurried by with their trucks, he turned his own way to the entrance.

The day passed by him with more trains and journeys to the coast and crossing of channels. In the greyness of sky and the green water lapping against the ferry, he thought of his old man.

By evening the motorway was black and he didn't have to look at anything except the lights and the drizzle on the windscreen as they charged up through the country. The wagon driver asked where he'd come from and passed over a smoke in wondering whether hitching was better at night.

"It's not bad" Jackie said, and mentioned that at least you could avoid the shit this way. The driver shook his head and pointed out the windows to where industrial estates and new towns were bathed in a landscape of greasy orange light. Lampposts shone down on broken glass and graffiti screamed in the empty streets. "You can never avoid that, no matter

21

when you travel."

The feelings stayed with him, echoing around in his head as Jackie walked the last miles from the motorway to the estate. The telegram was crumpled where it had been pushed into the pocket in Spain. It fell on the floor when he took his clothes off, and was still there next morning when his mother came in, her eyes all red and making a great effort to keep despair from flooding them.

She glanced at the creased paper on the floor and her face buckled, but still she wouldn't cry although tears were glittering in her eyes as the wind blew in a roar outside and banged on the windows from the sea. Liverpool was in her blood.

She said the daughter and the son in law were staying, and the relatives would be up later and they would all go to the church in big black cars, and then slowly as if searching for the next words she began to weep in bitter, futile tears.

After the church, they all went to the graveyard. It was cold and they huddled around cars until the priest came and mumbled words into the grave, as the drone of the bin wagons came and went to the nearby tip, and the seagulls wheeled above the piles of rubbish against the dark Merseyside sky. Their cries carried on the wind as people stood by the graveside, solemn or weeping into bunches of yellow and blue flowers they carried for his commemoration.

And Jackie stayed back at the house; comforted the old lady crying in her new black coat, made sandwiches when the relatives came back, cut the cake, kept the fire well stoked up and in the days that followed looked after the old man's mates who came up from where he used to work. And John Clare pulls him to one side and says " look after two things in life son; only two things, your health and your wallet"

This from a long time fighter on the docks and in the shipyards. Lungs ruined from the platers trade, hung over the side of ships in the cold and rain. An organiser from the time born and death is catching up with all around him, and he searches for things to say.

Jackie walks with him to the bus stop, slower now, where years before he had to run to keep up with the grey raincoat slung over the arm, and the scarf tied in the same old knot.

Jackie said he could have told him what a waste it all was and how the old man could have lived a lot longer, if he hadn't been ground down by work and insecurity and all the rest the working class has to live through from the day it is born. And John, old John, long enough a communist and battler with priests and relatives and wife who brought the kids up in the faith, shakes his head and says he knows all that; but he raises his glasses in the way Jackie remembered from that time back and his voice hardly needs to carry the words; "death comes anyway, Son."

And for the first time, stood with the older one by the bus stop in the rain and the wind snatching up sweet wrappers across the pavement, Jackie feels the lump in his throat and the tears start to rise, and he remembers the cold platform on the French border, and the young boy going home, and the lives in communities broken by people having to go away. And with his crying the older one takes his hand, and an arm is raised from frail shoulders to lay upon his own, and wait with him until the bus comes, all noise and red paint, to bear him home to his own empty house.

The old lady was in black clothes for a week. Then with cigarette blowing and kind of angry gusto, she laid them in a chest with mementoes from her war time marriage and dancing days, had a good cry, then cleaned the house from top to bottom and started back at work.

She did not need any more to remind her of his passing, as Jackie had no need of the stations at Cerbere.

What was gone was gone but the memories were stitched inside, the same as a wagon the colour of a bus that trundled him up the black motorway, in the night of his dead father, and the tales within of a cigarette smoking fighter of a driver.

BIRTHDAY SONG

Saratoga New York on T.V.
Afternoons from the 'Fifties.
Talking about Cafe' Lena
And the boys who used to know her.
Kerouac, Corso, Ferdlinghetti,
Lena without a daughter.
The whole Bohemian roadshow,
Drinking wine and forking spaghetti.

And the sun rides the brownstones
While they sang "Harlem River"
Fearsome on the waterfront
Where berths and piers turn golden.
Like September over Seaforth
With our Sunday parlour song,
By repair shops and half tide locks
And the Mersey's muddy waters.

The Old Man has one for us
As my Granny groans "Kathleen"
A bottle of Guinness for my Old Lady
Resplendent with new being.
And my Uncle Lenny wets the head
And starts for the door.
The Cunard Line this evening tide.
No video this of times gone by.
An ordinary side of Liverpool life.
That cafe's in New York.

SEVEN BELL BREAKFAST

Monday dawned humid and looked like rain. Joseph Murphy, chief steward without a ticket, who never went to bed less than drunk, opened his office. It was seven o'clock. He took a pair of heavily bound books out of the drawer and laid them on the table. Together with the fountain pen and a set of coloured pencils, they lay on the green oilcloth like remnants from an artist's still impression.

Murphy was wearing a striped shirt without a collar, fastened at the neck by a gold stud. Elastic braces half heartedly held his trousers up. A tall, spare man, he seemed to affect a certain look that rarely corresponded with the situation; a trifle vacant somehow. When he had the articles arranged before him however, his face took on a resigned but determined appearance. He sighed as he sat down, and gazed at the desk a moment, then took one of the pencils from its case and began to write. It appeared he wasn't thinking about what he was doing, but he worked with an obstinacy that belied his apparent absent mindedness. The pencil moved methodically down the squared pages as though possessed of a mind of its own.

After eight o'clock had been rung he paused in his work to look at the sea. The sun, behind grey blankets of cloud, shone down in sulphur coloured rays of light. Far away on the horizon the surface was a glassy yellow. He returned to his work with the idea that it would rain after breakfast. The voice of the cabin boy from behind the door drew him out of his abstraction.

"Hey Boss"

"What?"

"The captain wants you to take his tooth out."

"He wants to see the second mate." said Murphy.

He ran his index finger down the columns of figures he'd written, looking to see how they corresponded with those of the previous trip. "Paperwork" he muttered and cursed the unknown bureaucrats.

Outside in the alleyway, the cabin boy's voice called out

again. "The Captain says you studied medicine"

Murphy gave no indication that he'd heard. His lips moved silently. Only when the page was checked did he raise his eyes towards the door. "He knows that, does he?" The Captain must have been receiving messages.

He twisted the top off the fountain pen and dipped the nib into the bottle of ink. After filling it he replaced the stem and holding it between thumb and forefinger shook away any redundant drops of ink onto a sheet of pink blotting paper.

"Chief."

"Yes...what?" His face had resumed its old expression.

"He mentioned something about your brother."

"What about my brother?"

"He said he could help him."

He leant back and looked out of the port hole. The morning was still the same, hot and humid. He could already feel it's dampness in the armpits of his shirt.

"Tell the Captain I'll see him after breakfast" he said. He picked up the pen and began writing his figures over the faint pencilled markings.

When the boy brought him his coffee he was leaning back in the chair, a cigarette in his mouth.

"Boss." He set the cup down on the table,

"What?"

"Where's your brother now?"

Murphy turned his gaze away from the porthole and placed it on the enquirer.

"You ask too many questions."

"Is he in the nick chief?"

"Who told you that?"

"The cook did." The babbling brook, Murphy glanced in disapproval at the galley. Then relaxed. It wasn't worth getting angry with your cook. He nodded.

"Yes he's in jail." he said.

"Why?"

For Christ sakes, what did the kid want from him; blood!

"I'll tell you why" he said, his voice deliberately slow,

26

"then you won't have to ask again" He flicked the ash off his cigarette.

"Two years ago my brother was found with a woman."

"Is that all?" The boy appeared doubtful.

"That's all," said Murphy "now get out of here."

He reached down for the bottle he kept in a drawer beneath the table, and after studying it a moment, as if not sure, poured himself a good drink. Let the lad find out himself about the woman. The whisky soothed him and he lit another cigarette. He'd learn about that sooner than Communism. He looked out over the sea.

There was a knock and the Captain appeared in the doorway. He had shaved his left cheek but the other, looking painful and sore, wore a four day growth of beard. Murphy saw in his eyes the look of pain.

"Sit down Captain." he said.

"Good morning." the Captain said.

The chief sent the boy to get some boiling water from the galley, and when he returned poured some of it into a small tin basin. As he began to sterilise his instruments, the Captain rested his head against the back of the chair and began to feel a little better.

The office was very small. Besides the table and chair a narrow settee wedged beneath the port-hole formed the only other piece of furniture. The Steward went into the cabin to wash his hands. When he returned, the Captain looked up at him and leant far back in the chair, waiting to be examined. A warm, damp breeze came in through the opened port, and though it gave no respite as it blew over them, it provided a welcome change to the morning's stillness. As yet, it hadn't rained.

Muphy turned the Captain's face towards the light. After having observed the damaged tooth, he felt gently along the jawbone with a careful pressure. Satisfied, he stood back.

"You have an abscess." he said.

The Captain nodded as if he'd known all along.

"I haven't any drugs."

27

The Captain made an effort to smile.

"Worse things happen at sea."

The chief didn't say anything. Using a pair of tweezers he took the sterilised pincers out of the water and laid them on a towel that was spread across the settee. He placed a glass of water and a plastic bowl down beside them.

"You can use that to spit into."

He hardly looked at the Captain as he made his final preparations although the other's eyes followed intently his every movement. It was a lower back tooth of the kind dentists call number six. When he thought himself ready, the steward took hold of the pincers and inserted them into the Captain's mouth.

A moments hesitation as he searched for the infected area, then he clamped them gently around the tooth and stood with feet apart over the suffering man. Placing his hand over the Captain's shoulder he grasped the back support of the chair and held it there, firm.

"Are you ready Captain?" he asked.

Beneath him the master of the ship was almost numb with fear; a cold relentless fear that swept through his body making the perspiration stand out in large drops on his forehead and the feeling that some thing unknown was massaging his kidneys.

He held the chair tighter and forced his feet down hard against the deck, straining his will power to keep from moving as the pincers began to turn and the nausea rose up inside him. The steward's wrist did no more than make a movement that described a half circle. Without any rancour in his voice, even with a touch of tenderness he said to the Captain, "Ah Captain, if only Jerry could see you now."

And underneath him the Captain felt his jawbone cracking and his eyes filling with tears, but he remained firm in his chair. Then, with a tearing of the roots his tooth came out, and he slumped back, exhausted. When he saw it lying on the table still bloody, clamped between the pincers, it seemed so strange to him that for a second he remained confused. He

28

inclined his head toward the bowl and spat. Perspiration rolled in little rivulets down his face; jaded he fumbled with the jacket of his uniform and sought a handkerchief from the trouser pocket. The chief handed him a clean flannel. "Dry your face Captain" he said. The Captain did so.

He was still trembling. Whilst the steward was washing his hands he looked up at the ceiling. Somewhere between the strips of brown flypaper that hung down and had dead mosquitos clinging to them, he pictured his wife sat at a table writing to him. The letter he'd received over a year ago, telling him she was keeping the baby and going to live away. In the loneliness of his cabin, or worse when at home on leave, he often read it and wondered about his life.

The mosquitos spun slowly around as a puff of wind entered the cabin, and as they spun there was a peal of muffled thunder from far over the ocean, and the rain that had threatened all morning began to fall. The image blurred, and the ceiling returned to it's normal colour, and the steward was standing over him with a towel in his hands.

"Get some rest," he said "and wash your mouth with salt water after food."

The Captain stood up and straightened his uniform. With a last look at his tooth, he made for the door. Murphy watched him as he stretched his legs.

"What about my brother, Captain?"

"What about him?"

"You said you could help."

The Captain didn't look back. Closing the door behind him, Murphy heard his voice through the ventilation.

"He should have got ten years."

UP IN FRIESLAND

The wind was blowing across Friesland. It began early afternoon and went on through the night. As we crossed on the causeway from Den Over it blew in the fog off the sea, and it wasn't long after that the rain began. The cars had all turned on their headlamps and were creeping away across the water until they became lost in the swirls and hollow silence ahead. It seemed strange to see them like that, the water lapping at their wheels and their lights blazing, and it not yet two in the afternoon. And because you couldn't see across to the other side, you had the feeling they didn't know where they were going either, moving slowly like tentative insects, afraid, yet attracted to the web.

She screwed her face up and muttered something about it not exactly being God's country. I agreed it looked desolate enough. The wind, blowing wild from the North, drove the rain across wrecked barley fields and blackened trees and sensing its power, turned with a violent shriek towards the bridge, smashing and battering at the stanchions in an attempt to halt forever the uncertainties of the searching lights.

We were cold and didn't have much money, so we bought sandwiches and soup from a roadside hut and sat in a doorway out of the rain. The food tasted good. We were near the capital then, and all the lights were on in the shop windows, and people just finishing work were running for buses and trying to keep from getting wet. They didn't look as friendly as the ones in the South, but we never stayed long enough to find out. We took the bus for the country to look for a place to sleep. We slept out most nights.

Away from the coast the land was flat and very green, but the rain fell without cease and even the cows looked miserable as they watched us pass by. We were riding far down the bus, the packs on our knees and they gave us such sad, baleful glances, their eyes seemed to come right through the windows; then the steam closed over and they became no more than blurred images, their bells ringing, wandering in the mist and so much like ourselves.

She put her head on my shoulder and I smelled again that perfume she said she never used. Wearing my old raincoat, and a felt hat the rain had made damp and hung limp over her hair, she felt warm beside me. Something inside coaxed me to relax but I couldn't, and all the old uncertain fears crept back and rose inside me like yeast. I turned to her, wanting reassurance, but her eyes were closed now, her mouth slack and she didn't see me struggle, nor try to murmur half forgotten songs the dread of her leaving inspired.

She slept as the kilometres rolled by, and at last the driver looked in his mirror and nodded. When we had taken the bus at Leiuwarden I'd shown him a spot on the map and asked to be set down there. There was here now. I woke her. Seeing her struggle with the bags, he abandoned his schedule and waddled down to help us. He was fat and his face was red, and he looked portly in his blue busman's uniform. I stood at the side of the road and he passed the bags out, puffing as he threw the last one. We thanked him, and for a moment he looked like he was going to salute, but he never did. He must have been a regular driver on that run and the passengers accustomed to delays, because they all smiled or spoke to him as he went back up to his seat, and waved to us as the tyres hissed away. She waved back and the wind scattered the exhaust fumes across the road.

Ripkerk was the name painted on a signpost. We stood there a moment and took in the surroundings. The only houses were those sheltering behind the plane trees, rebuilt in red brick with their sills painted white, you could see through the leaves. The windows all had flowers in them, and looked down onto a narrow road that threaded away through a copse and out again through the fields, where a tractor was working, turning the soil that had once glowed with tulips in the spring of not so long ago. A flock of seagulls wheeled in the air above the fields and for a moment the war seemed a long way away. The wind brought their cries right back to us and somehow made the houses look even homelier, but maybe that was due to the cold and the drizzling rain and the feeling inside of not knowing.

In the west, the sky and land had joined and furrows like silent waves rode into the grey ridge of cloud. Around us the countryside was weeping, helplessly without hope, nor cause, like the tears of young children. Like strangers to each other we stood under a tree, our bags around us, smoking cigarettes, when a man appeared. He asked in English if we were lost. I shook my head but mentioned we had no place to stay. "Well, he said, and rubbed his beard, "There's an old school-house they don't use, no more than about a mile down the road. You could try there maybe." He spoke with an American accent. "Are you from the States?" she asked him. And he laughed and said No, he just lived there. "Sailed on the Lakes ever since the Depression. Canadian seamen's union, Michigan", he said. "And it's a damn sight colder than here in winter." He looked ruefully at his hands, "A damn sight". He'd missed the war out there on the old Lakes. "Just home now." His gaze fell away, as though he felt he should have been around.

We walked away in the direction he indicated and felt wet and wished we were inside. There was a dyke in the fields over to our left where a couple of sheep stood grazing, behind them and what looked a far way off, a farmhouse, isolated against the sky. The barn was built onto the back of the house and its black roof rose up and overshadowed the brickwork, sloped at each end to cover the walls. She gazed at it fascinated. "What is that for?" and I guessed and said it must be to protect it from the wind, which sounded reasonable enough, but wasn't. It could have been the rain, but I didn't feel like talking then. I felt her eyes on me and looked around, saw them skim away like a frightened rabbit. As if she knew what it was that troubled me. "What must winter be like up here?" She shivered.

"Hard", I said, and remembered the old man's barn was joined to the house, but it was smaller and built of stone and didn't look as prosperous as the ones up here. But I didn't tell her that, nor a hundred other things I wanted to say. The communism that would change all, but so often comes back to ourselves. And very quiet she was beside me. The rucksack rising and falling behind, buckled under an arm of the great, sodden raincoat. And the hair falls from under her hat, dark and damp and glistening with rain. She's staring into space with the kind of secret smile that never seems to break past the corners of her mouth, and leaves me the feeling that I'll never really know her. A voice inside me says, 'Forget it', you've been lonely too long.

We walked to where the trees broke and a solitary building stood back from the road. It was the type the Government had abandoned when they began to move the kids from the country to the big schools in the town; made of brick and timber, with a stone chimney, it's iron gutters were rusted and filled with weeds. Slates were missing from the roof and had been blown into the yard outside, and a beech tree grew beside one of the windows.

We had to cross the bridge over the dyke, and as we came away from the shelter of the trees the rain blew into our faces and sent us running for the door. It creaked as she opened it. "You go first," she said. I went inside and found a long, low room with wooden beams across the ceiling and plastered walls that were flaked and black with cobwebs. In the far corner was a stone fireplace. There were bird droppings on the floor and old newspapers scattered around, but the windows were sound and no rain came through the roof. I called out to her and felt easier now that we'd found somewhere to stay. She came through the door and smiled, and I put my arms around her and looked into her face. "It's been a lousy day."

"Yes, lousy." Her voice was strained. She turned aside and began rather hurriedly to pick up the newspaper and tidy the room. "I'll see if I can find some wood."

"Fran," her voice reached me at the door. "I think I'll have to see a doctor when we go back." She didn't turn around or look at me, and only the sound of the newspapers rustling as she gathered them broke the silence. I went outside.

Alone, the rain that had saddened me now became a form

of peace and, as the fear slunk away, it was replaced by a great calmness. Times would be better now. Perhaps a child, like an act of faith, would commit us, bind us in what we really felt but were too unsure of to say. Gone would be the uneasy silences. Her cryings in the night or whispering, Jack, Jack, Jack, the name of her dead father, as I lay in the half world between sleep and light. In the evening when she read, turning her eyes from page to wall, where they remained until the light in them died and the book was there again. So strangely sad, as if in the depths of her being there existed a hidden sorrow she herself was unable to comprehend, the pieces broken or lost. And later, in this contradiction to her smile she told me of past lovers she'd taken as she had grown older, and I tried to look calm, when really inside me was crumbling, and be so fucking liberal when I should have said, "Forget about them, you're here with me now. Stay."

The dusk was falling as I set off back. Returning home through the half light, my arms aching with the weight of the wood, I watched the shadows make dark imprints across the fields and above, the black, scarf like clouds as they scudded by. In the West, they were streaked the colour of lavender and rose and yellow above the watery sunset, pale in comparison with the others that bulged ominous and leaden in the far northern sky.

Coming close I saw the candle burning in the back window. The wind had grown stronger now and you could hear it in the trees and grass, and through the wires of the forlorn looking telegraph poles, stretching away down the sides of the road.

"Is that you Fran?"

I pushed the door open and found her inside, sitting, making cushions out of our blankets and with the last of the food spread on the ground sheet in front of the hearth. "Who did you think it was?" She looked up and gave a self-deprecatory shrug of her shoulders. "I don't know, it could have been anyone." The candle burned steadily behind her, and gave an added lustre to her hair that shone in the dimness.

God! Whatever made me come up here?" Her voice sounded tired, a little angry perhaps. But she seemed happier when we had the fire going. The light had gone now, and in the recesses and corners the shadows trembled on the wall and danced over the window.

We sat on the blankets and ate the food, and I took out the bottle from my bag and we drank it between us. There was a constant moan as the wind roared in the branches of the tree nearby, and across the fields and down the road to where an avenue of poplars shivered beneath the moon.

"I'm glad we're inside." The wine had warmed me and it felt good to be sat beside the fire. Overhead you could hear the rain falling on the roof, and the splutter of the flames when it came down the chimney.

"It's no night to be out in." I yawned.

"You're tired?"

"A little."

"I am as well." A nervous laugh.

I put my arm around her, and for what seemed a long time we sat and gazed at the fire, not saying a word, listening to the commotion of the storm outside.

"Fran." She looked away from the fire and her face was calm, almost impassive. "I'm going to have a baby."

There was a strange inflexion in her voice. Inside me, alarm bells broke into thoughts. "It doesn't matter," I said. "I'm glad. When I'm working we'll have money and there's the small place my Gran used to have in north Wales. The three of us can live there comfortably, no-one to bother us, long walks on the hills." My voice echoed my desperation,

She shook her head. "Fran, I don't know if it's our baby."

Her face changed, like a shadow from the fire, "I'm sorry, Fran, very sorry." I smiled and tried to speak, but no words came out. The names of her lovers seemed to be dancing on my tongue, and to say anything then would have been futile.

"Don't be angry," she whispered, "Please don't be angry." Her voice was soft and very low and came as if from a long distance, and it told me of a man and a sunny day, then of more days and the changing of the seasons and still the man, until his image filled the room and danced before me in the fire. The voice droned on, becoming ever softer, then it stopped and the silence came between us, and the only sound was the wind outside.

I sat by the fire and the candle burned low on the window-sill, alone with the ashes and the black roaring night. The last lines of the poem rose up inside and nearly choked me:

'In the prison of his days / Teach the free man how to praise' I still hadn't told her I loved her but that didn't matter now, nor even less when in the nether reaches of the night with the wind battering all around, she turned in her sleep and whispered, "Jack, Jack, Jack."

AN ANARCHIST'S TWILIGHT

The thought now burns like the summer sun inside me. I'll burn the place. I am sat here alone in the archives, the bales of crumpled paper around me that form my history and the long, lone fluorescent light bulb the assistant kindly left on, that shines a violet texture on to the flaked yellow parchments of the old newspapers.

No-one knows I am here. They have forgotten me. The basement where I am sat reading of my ancestors' mistakes, their tentative steps forward and their abject failures, has been officially closed hours ago. Before the porter goes around closing the rooms upstairs, I will have slipped quietly out into the night as is my custom.

They know me here now. They do not mind. Even if one did perhaps chance to come down here, what would he find? An old man dressed in a ragged overcoat and cap and silken muffler grimy with wear. The dew-drops dripping from his nose on to the cracked pages - could any harm be done by him? The one known as Wilfred, who has come here now so many times in his same old clothes. Sometimes he cries but he does it alone. There could be no harm in that one.

Only the other day one of the old porters mentioned that this tired place wouldn't see me nor him, nor any of us, much longer, and he clapped me on the shoulders. When I asked him why, he looked faintly startled and drew his hand back, unbelieving I had no inkling of the great event.

"Why, we're moving, Wilf...the whole seven storeys of us, lock stock and barrel over to the Central Library in town. It won't bother me," he added. "It gets into my bones in winter, this place."

Perhaps it was then that the half-image of what I might do crept in and lodged itself in a corner of my mind. It has taken until this time for the thought to come glistening to the surface. Louis Blanqui said that, but it doesn't matter. Can I help it now if my fingers suddenly start to tremble. I will burn the library. To see enveloped in angry flames, this edifice and mass of our misunderstandings, where the weak are led in whilst young and initiated before the altar. If only one human voice sighs with relief as the place comes down midst the crash of timber and the black engulfing smoke, then I'll know the job will have been well done.

These thoughts had their origins some years ago. It was a summer evening during the seamen's strike. I was walking along the Dock Road. The sun, casting long shadows across the derricks, and moving in crinkled pockets of light over the brown water, was lowering itself across the Mersey and shone in gold and copper on the lines and hulls of the unmanned ships. It had been a hot day. People in sweaty overalls, caps jolted back and carrying their evening papers, were returning home from work. A young seaman who recognises me, having stood for so long on picket duty on this, my old gate, gives me a wink and hands me the day's propaganda. The dust was rising from the wharfs. I thanked him and asked how his day had been. Boring, he said, and hot, hot as a bugger, yet perhaps if he'd read the poems in the pamphlet he held in his hand the weight of his standing may well have been lightened. German dockers were refusing to handle British cargo and their union had contributed to the pamphlet. In the form of a couple of small passages and the whole of an extract, was a poem by a man called Brecht. It was called 'The Sailor's Song'.

I can remember reading it avidly, although the lines escape me now. There was something about history judging us hard, yet no history recorded that was not distinctive to the few, those kings and great men for whom the millions toiled, but what of the millions, of their tears and sweat and dreams, would our children hear of them? Could there ever be a history that was not piecemeal, if their voice was excluded from the bellowing of the few? This touched me deeply.

It touched me deeply. I read the poem again and again, mostly at supper in the dark and sometimes lonely night, and in need of an audience, would lean on the after rail and recite to the water below. I was a ship's watchman, and although busy because of the strike and so much idle tonnage in the dock,

spent that summer reading the poet and his European ancestors. And then, perhaps then, with the summer having gone
and the strike broken up, and men after weary turns returning
to their ships, perhaps then was the faint spark of agitation
kindled in my old bones.

At this point, a mention of my past is worth recounting.
After many years of going to sea, I decided, in order to be nearer
home, to take up with the coasting lines and be able to spend
more time with my wife and rapidly growing daughter, both
of whom I loved dearly. I was a respected man, a captain. I
well remember the reaction of the crew as I first stepped
aboard in full and well-cut uniform, my cap straight and hair
and moustache carefully combed, with my family beside me
in full bloom, the little one holding tight on to my hand in awe
of the many ships and rushing feet. And the men, looking at
us as they lounged against the rusty accommodation of the
small vessel or twined ropes on the muddy and timber-strewn
decks, mugs of tea beside them steaming in the cold air,
looking at us and smiling. I must have cut a pretty figure as
I strutted the decks of my command, impressing my wife with
my talk and knowledge of ships and the river, and expansive
gesturing to accentuate various locations. No wonder they
laughed.

Little by little, the society of deep-sea sailing, in which I
had been steeped, throughout the fog of youth and manhood,
slowly began to disperse and in its place, in the hard winters
of the coasting trade, I came to see the men as if for the first
time. Perhaps the size of ship had something to do with it, for
in that small and fly-blown atmosphere, the loneliness and
division of the deep sea was only accentuated the more by the
enrichments of companionship. For too long I had suffered
my solitary responsibility. Now, together we sailed on many
trips. We drank. We sang. We walked down the streets of
Liverpool and Glasgow and Hull together.

All was not well at home. My wife, so dear to me throughout
our time, began to suffer me less and less. We quarrelled, I
swore. No longer could I stomach the fashionalia and

pretence of theatre and opera. At home, our lives were becoming separate. Sat in the comfortable leather armchair with an after-dinner glass of port, my insides would suddenly hanker for the noise and smoke of the bars, the clap of hands on shoulder and the singing out on the cobblestones. And many a time would I leave my unfinished drink, and with nary a word of explanation go out to wander across the city in search of companions. My uniform, once so prized, now lay forgotten in a trunk. No longer were there any pretensions on board. We navigated. We took the watches. Then came the gale.

We were returning from Glasgow with holds full of whiskey. Our ship pitching into the troughs. The wind was up and screaming, nothing was visible from the bridge, though we were not too far from home. We anchored, hove to into the teeth and hoped to ride it out. Come the morning, as the dawn opened over the spume and swell of the water, and the wind whipped grey banks of cloud across the sky, we found we had been dragged towards the banks at the mouth of the river. The rocks were up, sharp and black in the early yellow light. The anchor wouldn't hold. Behind the rocks and across an expanse of water creased with rising waves and spray, we could see the splinters of green moss, the beginning of the marshes, becoming clear out of the mist and away over, the first strips of sand. There was a sudden wretched scrape and rumble from within the holds and the entire vessel gave a lurch, the cargo had shifted and was turning us unbalanced, towards the rocks.

Something inside my brain told me that the gale wasn't so strong as its former self, but I dismissed the thought as we watched the rocks creep closer, their angry peaks drooling with foam. There was little time for discussion.

The order was given to abandon, on reflection perhaps too early, but no-one disagreed. In truth, we were all a little afraid. That stretch of the estuary is full of wrecks. We took to the boats and with everyone pulling, soon made the shore. I can remember looking, my face wrung with sweat and spray, and far away, seeing cattle graze on the inner marshes, knew that someone had to tend them, just as they had to tend to the sea, but at what great price, as we, with both gratitude and pity, watched our little ship flounder. Sometime after, we heard the groans and crash and splitting of timber as she hit the rocks, and then a little later, saw the first barrels come riding out of the hold and bob on the swell.

When we had thrown ourselves upon the sands, there was no one to be seen but now, some of the village people began to dot the beach and come down to join us at the water's edge. They cheered as one of the two local fishing boats came into view and made to guide our cargo safe to shore. How clear everything looked then, with the wind raging over the horse-shoe bank. There were the dark masks of our skeleton ship tilted against the grey sky and the sea, whitecaps rolling up onto the beach and seagulls wheeling and crying above the wreckage. But there were people. People now all around us, and excitement was in the air. The fishing boats had swung a net between themselves and were flushing the barrels shore-wards. There was much shouting and laughter.

At first I made some attempt to stop them carrying away their booty, but then I saw the futility of it all, and there was such a clamour with excited voices heard in every quarter, that it seemed stupid even to spoil their fun. Perhaps this went against me at the inquest. They said the gale was soon to blow itself out and the ship could have been saved. How were they to know? How was I to know?

It was a rude awakening to have my name in the papers and see the statement appear above the top of the column in bold black print, telling of my loss of command. It disturbed me that the enquirers - they are not called prosecutors in such genteel quarters as the Marine and Maritime Board - should look into, with such pointed interest, the effect of cargo and vessel, even though insured, to the scant attention they gave to the danger-ous conditions and the feelings involved of the people that sailed. The more sympathetic told me that I might sail again, as mate, once the affair had blown over, though it would be difficult on the coasting trade. I asked them why, and they tut tutted and hummed and said something about 'owners being loath', 'somewhat exceptional relations with the crew' and other such excuses that rapidly faded into an awkward silence. Perhaps I was too proud but I told them, no, never, not again would I take and give orders within that fraternity they represented. Needless to say, these latter lines were never reported, although columns were devoted to my besmirched name.

I took a job as a clerk in a shipping office. It was near the waterfront. Many times throughout the years I sat and looked over the river, and watched in winter the rain falling down on to the murky waters and the light shining out of the drizzle. Or in spring, the sunshine on the laden hatches with the men sitting and smoking and taking the fresh air with their afternoon tea from their slowly passing ships. Many's the time I wished I were back there with them. And tried to subdue my grief.

Lately, after my retirement, I have come by this watchman's job that provides the extra coppers to buy a drink. It is just the little things now. I am alone. My family left long ago. They could not bear the disgrace attached to my name, which was a pity, for I might have tried harder to convince them of the change. There it is then, that series of fragments of my past experience, that cannot fail but poke their nose into the present.

Before me I have a cracked embossed folder, and within it the five tattered newspapers whose editions carried my story. Whilst being not untrue - I gave the orders, my ship had sunk - they, in similarly fragmented and disjointed fashion, on whose statements my life had hung, did not present the whole picture. How many other articles and books are apt to do the same within our history libraries? Dismiss them and we shall see the future.

Now for days I have been bringing in my little bottles of paraffin and secreting them away behind some of the older files. The attendants will never find them, the place here is such a mess that nobody bothers to tidy any more. You can see they are preparing for an early exit. The sooner the better, they tell me. It'll be sooner than they expect but, my God, some of these old records are heavy, the assistants only touch them at their utmost need. The enormity of the task is not only mental. It has cost me no small exertion to place my little bottles behind the volumes, and many a time I must sit quite still - after lifting a particularly voluminous bale of old rubbish - and calm my thumping heart.

Often in the past, when something particularly pleasing had caught my attention, such as the sun over the water, it seemed the right thing to do to sit down and watch and think of nothing much and perhaps smoke. Yet when the time to depart had come, with the sun gone lower and the cigarette a smouldering butt between my tired fingers, I felt somehow empty and dissatisfied and the slow, bitter taste of tobacco would rise in my throat with the nothingness. How different my feelings now in preparation. How different the pleasures of smoking after my little bouts of exertion. There is the sudden purpose. My time is not far away.

The days have slipped by like shadows and the plan is set. This evening I have remained down in the basement; hid when the porter comes to check, watched him switch off the lights before leaving. That was some time ago. Above me I can hear the footsteps on the stairways, soon they will all be home.

The bottles have been emptied. The paraffin spread carefully over the walls and floor. I take up a torch from the table, and lighting it and holding it at arms' length, carefully set fire to the old books, the withered documents, and embossed volumes. Like the reaction from the philosophy they expounded, all will soon go up in smoke. Everywhere is now slowly burning, slowly and then a little more. Burning.

I stand and watch the flames a moment. Two moments, three, I must go, they are rising. What does it matter, the deed is done. I could stay here and like the parchments, burn alongside them. No, says a voice, go, just go, escape, get out of here. The deed is done. The smoke begins to waft upwards in blackened puffs. I make the fire exit.

I tug on the bars, the old bars fixed across the wood. They won't yield, I tug again. Behind me the flames are inching their way up the wall. A cold wave of perspiration sweeps over me. I kick and tug at them with frenzied gasps. It's no use. They won't give. I recollect the phrase 'death-trap' from an earlier conversation with the old porter. 'Death-trap, death-trap,' the words keep ringing in my brain. I give one last futile effort, nothing will budge them. The sweat drips from my hair and runs down between my shoulder blades. Turning, I see the flames alight upon the stacked books. They relish the taste of paper. Their long tongues are feasting upon the printed word and making crackling noises that are accompanied by sudden bursts of green and blue sparks. The longer flames form an angry welt of orange, spread the length of one wall. I cover my face with the collar of the old overcoat and stumble through them, my relics forgotten on the table, to the opposite door that leads to the stairs.

The night is dark outside the windows. They are high up from the street. It is too far, too far down, I must not panic. I draw up a chair and sit, looking out of the great glass pane. Beneath me I can hear the rumble of the thing I set in motion. Belatedly I think of my small mementos that were part of me. Part of my life. The smoke comes spiralling up the staircase. I feel exhausted. People are on the street. People to touch upon. Nausea sweeps over me.

They have gathered into crowds down there. Many fingers are pointing, some are beckoning. A sea of faces is looking upwards. Around me books are burning everywhere. The flames are licking up the stairs creeping through the floor-boards from the furnace below. One hundred years have been obliterated. Theses have been postponed. Professors are weeping. Students must look elsewhere. The people must be told. The sheer grinding monotony of slow conversation, each and every day for a hundred years. We must go forward. We must go forward.

In the distance I can hear the fire bells. The engines will soon be here. A sudden rush of crackling and air and the floor is alight behind me. People below are shouting and beckoning. I am still sat by the window. I stand up. What use is there for me in dying. My cheeks are streaming with the smoke. I am not too old. This is my beginning. My explanation must have its being here. I take up the heavy wooden chair and hurl it through the window. As the pane smashes a murmur ripples through the crowd. Voices go up like caps in the air. I climb out onto the ledge and see the engines and the police as they come hurtling and blaring around the corner of Paradise Street, strangely near to my old cafe.

The light has dawned. Is it me then, really me, one who has been so quiet throughout the years, who is now bellowing the words: 'Comrades' to the people below. They shall hear my explanations. Walton Gaol will ring from wall to wall with them. Converts will be gained. I slip and fall, aware of a sudden ghastly wrench, a swift passage through the air. A figure bends towards me and quickly looks away. The crowd stand back. I am alone. The blood runs along the pavement. "Tell the papers", I whisper.

THE CONNECTIONS OF BILLY DONAGHIE

A couple of days before John Lennon was shot to death in New York, someone told me that Billy Donaghie had died. The only connection is that they both came from the South End of Liverpool, one closer to the water than the other, if you know what I mean. And Lennon was not the first, and won't be the last Liverpudlian, to be killed in the Big Apple. Plenty have died there, but they have generally been seamen, and no-one writes much about them, except a few lines about how they died near the waterfront; many lines will be written about Lennon and who could argue. Anyone who could write songs like 'Imagine' and 'Working-Class Hero' deserves to be written about, but I wonder how many lines will be written about Billy Donaghie. He wanted to write a few himself, but died before he had the chance. He was in New York once upon a time, but you have to go back a few years for that. It was in 1927 that he first started going away to sea, and one of the first things his father told him was to stay clear of the union. Not that his old man was prejudiced against organisation, but he saw the seamen's union as just being a company shop. Not many would have disagreed with him at that time; any grass root action or campaign was invariably smashed, and it was only a year since the General Strike when alone the seamen were instructed to remain at work by their autocratic President General Secretary. Indeed, the Liverpool officials were all suspended from office for heeding the call of the TUC.

There was another reason as well. Billy was born in the heart of the 'Orange' area of Liverpool and there was a long tradition there of local control. It originated from the small docks of the South End, with the little streets winding down on to the dock itself. Parochial wasn't the word. Billy remembered many twelfths of July, when Catholic shops would have windows broken and 'the old woman who sold fruit would have her barrow overturned by the mob'. Catholics were the 'coggers' and he was told to stay clear. He remembered these divisions when he first went away to sea, how his friend was a Catholic, how when he had an accident Billy went to see him in Sussex Street, only a few hundred yards from his own household, yet being scared stiff someone was going to set upon him. And later, sat in the parlour with a bottle of brown, still thought of what awaited him outside. He spoke often of the way people were segregated and fenced off, and he witnessed it again in many different ways on the ships that sailed out of Liverpool in the 1920s.

They were days when North and South Ends of Liverpool were almost separate enclaves, and then again, enclaves within that often isolated and split by tensions as they all bowed beneath the weight of the Depression. Times when Southern men still regarded the Harrison boats as their own, and kept up a bitterness towards other sailors from the North End. The docks were worse, with casual labour the over-whelming insecurity of existence resulted in a language of 'what school did you attend?' as the most important arbiter of work.

It was these barriers that made Donaghie rebel. But like so many others he had to go beyond Liverpool to do it and make it stick. He did what many other seamen before and since have attempted, in ways to express their freedom and their resentment with the lack of any say in the running of the ships, and the lousy conditions. He jumped ship. The first time was in the States, and used to this phenomenon, they sent him straight back to Liverpool. After a period of time he sailed again, and this time had more about him. He 'backed out' of his ship in Canada, then rode around a bit on the trains before 'beating the border'. He stayed in the States some years this time, and eventually married there.

It was in the States that he first actively tested politics, joining the last of the Wobbly meetings and talking with others about how the movement had broken. He himself had worked in timber mills from where much of the radicalism had come. Dangerous to be seen too much on the streets in New York, an illegal immigrant and political activist, he would talk

47

in cafes on the Lower East Side with others, communists and anarchists of every political dimension and nationality. They would meet at the harbour, hold meetings, talk and drink with the seamen whom they knew, as there were always ships coming in from Liverpool. Fond of saying that others thought of him as a born rebel 'it was circumstances that made me rebel, kid', he would state in as firm a tone as you would ever hear from him. Circumstances brought him home to Liverpool and the Dingle in the middle of the 1930s. No picnic that; but he'd left the States because the going was even tougher; no streets of gold there, with a wife and two small children.

Hanging around Liverpool; no ships to join, not with his record. He haunted the South Docks looking for pick-up work. One or perhaps two days a week scattered here and there. Twelve bob a shift and the rest on the UAB.

It was a relative who was 'a boss' in ship-repair works and lived in the same street that brought him his first regular job after he had been on the dole 16 months. 'Me uncle was on for Harland and Wolfe, a good bloke, but like all of them, he took the ale for getting you on. Me, I didn't have to pay but others did, good like, but a stooge in the system.' Work was in the Harlow Street area of the Southern Dock, a noted Orange thoroughfare. Billy was soon shop steward in the local General and Municipal Workers, yet he could remember Houseman, the Tory MP and Orange, coming around these streets in the same Depression years and being cheered to the echo as he went by in the car. 'Only a few people put Labour posters up, and they got murder for it.'

Discriminated against for not working overtime through the night after a full days shift, he was warned that next time would be the last when he urged workers to leave their night work to vote in the local council elections. Voting was more important than working day and night just to fill the order book and then be laid off, but the employer didn't think so and neither unfortunately did many workers.

When the War came he was working intermittently for the Ellerman and Papayani shore gang. He left to join the army and serve with the artillery overseas, lucky in this case not to still be a seaman and sailing the convoy ships. His mates in the merchant navy suffered death more than any other workers in these years when Liverpool was the heart of the Western Approaches.

After the War, he continued his long career on the waterfront with work on the salvage boats, shore gangs and the docks themselves. He remembered the salvage work on the 'Thesis' sunk in Liverpool Bay; about how the money was so good, the best he'd had, but what conditions they had to accept in return. As ever, he wouldn't pay the price. In 1948 the year he began work as a registered docker, he was recruited into the Communist Party by Jack Coward, a fellow seaman and Spanish War veteran. It was with that party that he stayed up until his death.

He fought on many campaigns, notably the one around the 'Dockers' Trial' of 1951, where many past antagonisms in the port were settled and although sacked the following year, returned in 1957 to help heal breaches opened up in the bitter warfare of the Liverpool union in the 'blues' and 'whites' of the mid-fifties.

In between times, there was work on the shore gangs and even the tug-boats, though an officious superintendent and an order to paint the funnel on the afternoon of Christmas Eve soon put paid to that. After many months without work he again returned to salvage work on the 'Ranger', and as he came to join the ship a group of workers took hold of a red flag and waved him aboard with it, singing and shouting as he came up the gangway. They knew him as a 'commo', but they knew him even better as a fighter and that was always to be respected.

Reinstated again to the docks, he again became involved in the ever-present and consistent fight against the system of casual labour which had led so many times to his own dismissal. Throughout these campaigns he was known not only as a good speaker but a most meticulous organisation man. Too honest for his own good, noted Frank Deegan, in his autobiography 'No Other Way' about a lifetime of struggle on the Liverpool docks, 'In 1959 I had been elected treasurer of the Port Workers Committee, the previous treasurer had been victimised over a paltry dispute and sacked from the industry. Billy Donaghie had performed this task with much zeal. He was as honest as the day is long; so straight was he that he wouldn't even fool the employers, which was something I had no qualms in doing. He would never expend any money unless he gave or received receipts and he regularly issued statements of accounts. I decided to follow his example.'

It was ironic that after he had fought yet again against his dismissal and had come back to speak at the 1960 meetings concerning relations between the Liverpool and London dockers, that he should have to retire prematurely from the docks some months later. The doctor informed him he had chronic bronchitis - a disease well recognised by those who have worked within the dockers trades, but scarce acknowledged beyond. The last years of his working life were kept up with the union and the party as he worked as a lift-man in the Cunard Buildings down by the Pier Head. When he retired, he put all his efforts into the Transport and General idea of having regular trade unionist and retired workers' meetings. For many years he was secretary of the Merseyside Trade Unionists' and Pensioners' Association and fought and publicised on all the issues, of a better deal for those who had worked all their lives and now were suddenly alone. He was still secretary of this organisation when he died.

At a personal level, his last years, instead of being easy, were harder than most. His son, who had not been able to find work for many years, was still living at home after an unhappy marriage, and was in Billy's terms, 'An early victim of the system and of the doctors who do the clearing up with their easy giving of drugs.' He himself was suffering increasingly with his lungs, especially in the winter, and their flat in the Dingle almost on the waterfront itself, had to be constantly kept warm, especially the front room where he worked.

Then came the time when I went to visit and found the flat

all boarded up. There had been an explosion; a gas pipe that ran beneath the floor and of which they had often complained, so much so that they had changed to electric, had exploded, severely injuring his wife and making them move out. He wrote to me apologising for my wasted visit, in his usual meticulous and polite way. The shock of the explosion, however, combined with the earlier run-down of his wife's health, which had left her partially paralysed, and concern about his son, all took their toll. When I next saw him, they were living in one of the high rise blocks that gaze over Sefton Park, which the council had temporarily allocated to them. The rent was as high as the floor on which they lived and his lungs were worse; it took him a long time to open the door, yet still stood in the corner was the old typewriter and the bundle of correspondence and literature concerning the pensioners' struggle. It was the last time I was to see him, and he still had the fire in his eyes; what he wanted most now was to write a book, a good book about his time as he talked over the travels and the struggles that had framed his life. Unfortunately death wouldn't allow him that, just as it denied John Lennon on the eve of his new beginning. Lennon once said that 'They knocked me for saying Power to the People and that no one section should have the power. Rubbish. The people aren't a section. The People means everything. I think that everyone should own everything equally and that the People should own part of the factories, and they should have say in who is the boss and who does what. Students should be able to select teachers, it might be like communism but I don't really know what real communism is.' Billy would have agreed with these sentiments and although he fought for communism all his life, life had also taught him the art of struggle within organisations and that really was his true strength.

His early years with the seamen had taught him that necessity and most of all, the way angry shouting could become just as many words broken on the wind, if not channelled in a constructive way.

John Lennon had to go to the States just as Billy Donaghie

had done in his different way and as so many others from Liverpool have done before and since, most of them not living in plush apartments, but that's by-the-by, for in the end, it guarantees no safety. The waterfront is not such a different world after all, and it has been the source of Liverpool's strength in more ways than one; whether Lennon would have come back to it cannot matter now and his death brings sadness to us all, but Billy Donaghie is also dead and the many who knew him will be all the poorer for his passing.

THREE MEN IN ANORAKS

The 'Coffee shop' looked closed - but it wasn't. Just because it had steel shutters up around the windows didn't mean to say it was closed - the lady told us that. She also told us the way to the job centre. Most people know that in Garston.

A couple of blokes wandered over and gave the once-over to the new jobs that appeared in the window of the old dole. Big bold hand-written letters proclaimed a roofing assistant's job at forty quid a week. MUST BE ABLE TO WORK HEIGHTS, the notice ran on.

The office opened and the people went in out of the cold. In no time there was a crowd sat in the far room for the reception. Back on the notice boards where the jobs had been set up on neat typewritten cards, a couple of young people mooched about. A pale girl clutching a handkerchief; a lad with his mother. The office bright and warm. Nothing doing.

Less on the Estate

We started to look around the boards. The skilled sections had the most. There were about ten fitters jobs and then only a couple that spanned the range of miller, turners, borers and grinders. As usual the best money was for faraway places with strange sounding names. The money was lower on the estates and it was pennies for jobs in the city. The going rates for sparks could be £20 different between working in Broughton and working in Liverpool. There were about a dozen jobs going for electricians so the cake wasn't so big anyway. A notice at the bottom of the cards said "Vacancies for drillers, fitters, sheet metal workers and turners in other parts of the country would attract a special government allowance." You had to ask behind the desk for that one.

Three wise men in anoraks waltzed in for a browse. One of them pointed to a job in Saudi Arabia. £230 a week. The others looked at him.

"Th's for a plan manager"

"Y'get yer arm cut off on the ale"

"Robbers get stoned"

"Be no good for dockers"

They went out in the cold. Leaving the posh plants and the blended open plan furniture behind. You could see the assistants were only trying to help. But the boards had a story all of their own.

There wasn't anybody looking at the clerks and typists section. But there seemed plenty of vacancies, along with other bits and pieces of white collar work. The money never went beyond sixty and mostly was around forty. And then there was part time work. When we left there was a women with a baby looking through. Her husband was over by the building trade board that read like a horror comic. A few jobs for joiners, one or two for pipefitters, a couple for bricklayers. Nothing for labourers. Cherchez la cash and you'd have to travel.

And Leece St. was much the same. Tasteful decor - lots of people and even less hope. The women in charge saw us taking notes and came over: "We get all sorts in here", she explained "It would help if the management were informed. Maybe they could help" she said. "You wouldn't believe what some of them get up to." She flicked her hair nervously. "Some only come in for a laugh." Somehow the joke was lost as people gazed at the boards.

Outside the wind was kicking up the papers along the street. And the buses were packed with people bound for Netherley and Belle Vale. It was two o'clock and the beer was going up next week. In the pub the boss was moaning about the strikers. There was nothing left to do but to sink a few before you sank yourself.

THE SEAMEN'S STRIKE, LIVERPOOL

So you've come to stand on the stones of the dock road, the warehouses shimmering in the sunlight and throwing shadows across the water where the rubble of the Wirral rises out beyond the locks, and you hold up the placard in your hand as an odd lorry goes by and kicks up the dust. And you look over at the ships all laid up in their berths and think of how dead they look, no more than iron hulks without the men. And the coppers watch you from their hut as you stroll up and down and try to remember how it all started and it's funny that you can't, can't remember anything up and down on the picket line each Friday as though you'd been doing it all your bloody life. Then you remember the song, the only bloody song he ever knew and you picture him that night with his hair blowing and his fists up and him saying don't let them fool you and the song of the 'Saints' going rolling around the deck and getting lost on the wind. And now it's a quiet afternoon in late May and no-one goes down to the ships any more and the strike is two weeks old and still the song keeps dancing in your head.

And you mind that time the year gone by, homeward bound and two weeks from Liverpool and the football on the wireless and the mess room below deck where the lads had gathered with their mugs of tea and tins of baccy, and the smoke drifting up surrounding the bulwarks and being cut by the plum voice of the world news that tell you all seamen are to get a big rise within a few weeks. And Joe Conlan smiled that funny way he had of crinkling up his big face and turned to his donkeyman mate, and you hear him say they'll want something back for that. And Wally Jolly nodded the way he did when he'd finished telling you anything important, like the way donkey men got their name for having to lug their own mattresses down to the ships in the old days, and nodded again. You look out beyond the deck and see the sun flitting across the crests as the after end dips and rises in the late afternoon and the masthead a moving shadow along the water and inside the swirl of voices and shouts as Liverpool go one up, and you thought about the extra few bob and what Conlan meant about them wanting something back.

You soon found out. You had to work seven days a week now before overtime. Then the union bloke took some papers out of his briefcase and showed you what the agreement had been, and a couple of lads told him that ever since they'd gone to bloody sea the story had been to fight for less hours not more and didn't they have us enough by the balls already? The union bloke shrugged and you got the feeling he wasn't so happy either, but he didn't say anything. Mates and Masters could now turn you out any time they wanted to, weekends away were to be just the same as any other day, the big rise had taken care of that.

Months passed. Eddy Judge would sit in his cabin and stare at the radio that gleamed back at him from the small alcove. The radio with all its little buttons and switches and smell of leather meant more than anything when he was away. When his watch was finished he'd sit and fiddle with the dials, listening to the different bursts of music and snatches of foreign voices that kept him in touch somehow. The Yankee services station was the best when you touched the Caribbean. Eddy had a girl once in Granada who'd play the same tunes. She used to call for him on Sundays down at the Quay and off he'd go, showered and shoes shining, running down the plank and waving to those bastards spending their lives doing overtime out on the deck. Magic. The radio played on, Eddy wondered why she didn't come any more and why he had so little time free, he felt his hands go tense as he fiddled with the dials and the music came roaring out. It wasn't enough for them to have you on their bloody ships all of your life, they wanted all your days to boot. He switched the set down and, suddenly still, thought about the little bit more they were chiselling out of him.

You'd sit there with Eddy and Sid Fletcher on cold nights when you were all on the same watch and listen to the wireless, or when with a few bevies you got Sid going and he'd tell you about times when he was a boxer, and poor Sid, you knew by the way his face would twitch that he'd been knocked around. Sometimes he'd bunch up his big hand until you saw the broken knuckles white against the skin, and pound it down on the table so the whole cabin shook and only the radio would be playing soft, and Eddy would say take it easy mate, and Sid would just give a little shrug of the shoulders.

The big hours started the trouble. Bloody Sunday in Durban harbour where you can look over and see the waves crashing on the bluffs and people out on the beach surfing and having a good time, and there's a shout from the far end of the companion way and you can see the mate and the skipper grabbing hold of Sid. Poor Sid with his shoulders giving that little twitch, and a vacant look in his eyes you sometimes see in people that are deaf. And Paddy Hayes comes running from out of the galley and tells you he's just given the chief engineer a clout. And the firemen come up in their clean clothes saying the second had knocked them off for the afternoon but the chief had changed his mind. They were all off to the beach when he calls them back and tells them there's a job below. It was after that Sid went up to see him, and the engineer starts shouting about him being in the officers' mess and Sid starts twitching and it was all over in a couple of seconds.

And they put Sid in jail for that and kept him there a month until another homeward bounder could take him back to England, and it wasn't worth the trouble by the time the skipper had logged him for every penny he was worth, and blacked him down on the federation so that he couldn't sail again. The lads called a union meeting next day, and you heard the chief steward had told his lads not to go, and one of the pantry boys was going to be made into a rating next trip and the steward called him to one side and told him if he wanted the job he'd better not make that meeting; but they were all there when the time came.

The South African union bloke said there was nothing we could do. Sid had committed a mutinous offence and was in jail; the best we could claim for was to change him from the nigger to the white jail. And some of the lads thought that was terrible, Sid being jail with all the blacks, but then Mattie Hynes got up and said what the fuck jail does it matter, he's still there. And you thought of the dockers, who were brought to the ports, digging in the waste bins for bits of scraps and bones covered with custard and tea leaves and alive with flies, and you thought those bastards weren't having such a time of it either. Then Eddy gets up and starts on about them being able to make you work Saturdays and Sundays, and what's happened with Sid was all because of that. And you wonder whether he was thinking of the woman when he goes on about how we're all wasting our lives in this bloody game, and even Joe Conlan starts to nod, then a couple of lads tell him to calm down because all his shouting won't do Sid any good.

And you got wiser after what had happened and as the weekends came and went, you didn't expect any time off any more, but the buggers weren't going to get any more out of you than you could help. The lads loaded up with rum from Barbados that next trip, and Saturdays and Sundays you'd always have a few. And you'd put down your cloth or brush and roll a smoke and get your mate to keep nooky while you dipped down below for another wee glass, and they couldn't touch you as long as you were there on the deck between the twine and the boom and the creaking winches.

Back at sea you took it easy, and thought about what had happened to Sid and all the others, and on the way home as you crossed into the Atlantic and the swell got bigger and the days turned grey, you sat down in Eddy's cabin and talked about different things and the people you'd known, and listened to his radio as the wind blew outside. One time when he turned to the World Service, you heard that the union weren't too happy with the way we had to work weekends without overtime or any choice. And Joe Conlan shrugged and said if they felt like that why had the bastards agreed to it in the first place. And Eddy shook his head and got out the last of the bottle.

At home you got the drift of the way things were moving down in the union. And you heard that most of the Liverpool lads wanted to get back to the original demand of the forty-hour week, and Conlan raised his face out from his glass and wiped the Guinness away from his whiskers, and said they'd been talking about that since the time he was away. And you kept quiet, what with everything that had happened the last year and because you were still the youngest and knocked about when the others went home to their wives, and you bore it in mind without really knowing what way you were thinking, except that it didn't pay to crawl.

Then you were sailing wide down the Caribbean, and the days passed in song and the nights a blur of music and drink and you forgot about yourself and your thoughts, and the skipper hadn't turned out so bad, and Saint Lucia and Saint Kitts and Antigua and Barbados passed like a dream. Then into the blue harbour of Granada, and Eddys' girlfriend came down one night in her car and took a crowd of you away up beyond the scrub, the water glistening below and you with your bottles of rum, dancing in the whirl of the clubs. And someone gave you something to smoke which made your head go light, and you felt good by god and looked in the mirror to see if your face was twisting up the way it felt, and you didn't want to know about anything except nights like these with dancers swirling in long dresses and flowers in their hair; and you got up and sang and did your little piece and people laughed, you saw their faces in the dark, and Eddy's girl had her eyes closed and was dancing with him slowly, and the rum kept flowing and you didn't know what you were smoking any more. And the next morning with your head like a bell and a stomach that seemed to stretch to your knees, Paddy Hayes calls you in for breakfast and as you tram down the deck your little hat askew and sweat streaming everywhere, he tells you the union have called a strike.

Homeward bound you hear that the Prime Minister is going to speak to all of you on the radio, and you go down to the mess room with the crowd and sit next to Cavanagh and Hayes who's come from the galley and tells you that the officers' mess is full, and every bugger there that a strike wouldn't affect anyway.

The voice, rich and deep, of the World Service man announces the broadcast and at that instant the room goes quiet and blokes pull up their chairs and some clear their throats as if they are going to do the talking, and next thing you know Wilson's slow Yorkshire accent comes filtering out over the room in such a tone that you think the sea is going to turn back or something. And it goes on and on telling you what good fellows you all are, and how the nation is in debt to you and at this time of crisis you are more than valuable. You can see some of the lads nodding and others just sitting there quiet, and then the voice tells of the harm a strike could do and the margin of the balance of payments, and that the seamen of this country don't want to hold the nation and a Labour Government to ransom by their action; and the voice trails on and on until it fills the room and seems to come out of every stitch of wood on the bulwarks and has everyone rooted, until its presence slowly fades and there is a silence in the mess.

No-one said a word, and blokes if they looked at you simply raised their eyes or gave a little smile, and it was hard to know what anyone was thinking. Some scraped their chairs against the deck and others started to roll smokes, and one by one they started to drift away; you got the feeling somehow the message had sunk in, and no-one knew what to do so they smiled or smoked to hide their silence.

Then a funny thing happened some days later; Eddy sang his song. There was a party for the pantryboys birthday and everyone brought their cases of ale, until they spilled over and filled the deck of the spare cabin. Blokes were perched on the double bunks and others brought in stools and one, searching for an opener, pulled the locker doors ajar, and there stood on the top shelf were half dozen bottles of bacardi some bugger had filched away. Someone said it was a good omen and you sat there chasing the spirits with a can of Tennant's lager, watching the smoke get thicker and the songs louder until the bosun came knocking that he can't get to sleep. Then someone has got hold of a box and fixed a brush pole to it with cord and is playing the bass, and another's brought out the spoons and everyone breaks into 'the sash', and you all go trooping down the alleyways, limping and laughing and blowing on imaginary flutes the way they do for the orange parade. And out on the after end with the wind blowing and clouds riding like mountains across the moon, you start up again and the lads coming off watch join in and cabins are ransacked for any last drop. Then when the heads are rolling and the bass has gone quiet and the only sound is the ocean roaring down the runnels and the odd clink of the spoons, Eddy weaves himself up onto the hatch, his hair blowing wild and hands dangling by his side like you see in the movies, and he's mumbling something about all us poor bastards throwing our lives away, and then starts singing the only rebel song he ever knew and his head's shaking as the 'Saints Go Marching' billows around the deck; and you're all up on your feet giving it the last turn, and he's balled that big hand up into a fist before you and as the strains glide off into the night he's waving it above his head and shouting over the wind, don't let them fool you, don't let the bastards fool you.

The song kept dancing around in your head all the way home, and come the middle of May, Liverpool had rolled in from where you anchored on the river, and you could tell even in those early days there was a strike on by the way unloaded ships were being laid up in the berths. And after you'd come through the locks and been paid off you went up through the gates, your bags in hand and passed the lads on the picket with bloody stupid banners in their hands, and you thought they wouldn't have you doing that; then you were up in the union a week later and they said they needed someone for the MacAndrews gates down in the south end; and before you knew where you were you were standing with the board by the quiet dock: the coppers watching you from their hut and the odd lorry passing, and driver sometimes waving as he kicked up dust.

The days went by slowly, broken up by returning ships and you'd meander along to see if you knew anyone paying off, and maybe get a drink and a few smokes. And you knew the union was organised; every day they'd have a crowd up there and have them registered and have the pickets out, and while you still had a few bob you'd hang around. And sometimes you'd cross Canning Place and have a drink in the 'Customs House' that Cavanagh's Auntie Nell used to run, and when the money ran short she'd let you have a few and pay her when you could. And the days dragged by into weeks and you kept on doing your turn, stood down on the gates, watching the ships strung side by side across the water and you'd never seen so many in the docks before, it made you wonder how many blokes were just like you, with the sun pouring down and the dust getting into your eyes as it blew the length of the miles from the north to the south end of the docks.

And you met Ronnie Ferguson one day, and the two little kids he had with him were whining until you felt like kicking them, and you bought them ice cream if only to keep the little buggers quiet and thought, pan lids, who'd have them. You went back with them for a cup of tea and as you walked in you knew something was up, the curtains drawn even as the sun was shining and three other children sitting in the gloom, the smallest on the wife's knee. The baby made little whimpering noises and her little body seemed to shake all over, you looked at the woman's hand, red and furrowed as she brushed her lank hair away from her face, and saw her look quiet like as Ronnie went out to make the tea, and called after him there was none, and no supplement till Thursday. He looks as if he's going to shout, you see the red come up in his face but then he drops his eyes and the wife turns away, tired, and strokes the kids as another starts whining and Ronnie shoos them out onto the street.

You get the eldest to bring some tea from the corner shop and the wife takes a smoke, and it's rising round the stinking room with the sun cracking the flags outside, and she asks how long will it last, and you say you don't know and Jesus you hadn't reckoned on anything like this, and look from the linseed cloth on the table to the worn lino and the fuggy smell of the bedrooms and the clothes the kids were wearing. You could imagine at night in this heat with the kids whimpering and moving and scratching on the mattresses, and Ronnie next to his worn woman and her thinking what to feed them all with, the lousy few bob from the union and the odd shillings from the supplement. Him with his kids down on the picket, anything to get them from under her feet, and it was bad enough when he was away but at least she had the nights to herself then. Ronnie with his brothers coming home drunk with a few groceries wrapped up in newspaper, and Jesus she'd be better off dead than on strike. What would happen if women went on strike? You make your move and leave your fags and go through the door, and take big breaths in the street with the houses knocked down both ends and the kids on the brickfield, and you thought bugger that for a game, who'd have kids. You thought of a few others things as well.

One day you hear that there's an investigation been made about the seamen. And the papers are full of it and this Justice Pearson is doing such and such and the government shared his view, yet the hours weren't going to drop much; and you read about the way seamen shouldn't be sent to prison for missing their ship any more, and you remembered poor old Sid. And a few of the lads are saying they can put their reports where they like, and Joe Kenny of the executive tells you the same when he comes down on the gates and you know he's all right, and a few others join in. And up in the 'Woodhouse' you sit there and have the crack, and get the feeling you're going somewhere and not let the bastards down on the pool forget it. Then Joe gets up, tells you we're going to win this one and they're not going to have us by the bollocks anymore, and the 'hear hears' ring around the walls and some of the dockers out for their dinner-time pint stick a couple of quid down for the next round, and a lad that's with Joe looks as pleased as punch and starts on about solidarity and all that crap, and you think back to the Ferguson's house and how solid they were; so solid they were driving each other crazy and it made you wonder.

And another week went by and they still gave you a few free rides on the buses, and some of the dockers that worked your berth might give you the entrance fee to the pub; and every now and then Nellie Flanagan would pull one for you, and you thought this was going on all over the town, and maybe on the docks all over the country and Jesus, wasn't that a game, and you remembered the lad from the pub with his words of solidarity and you knew they were a lot of crap, but it was funny the way they kept coming back.

That week you read in the papers that Secretary Hogarth has said that seamen could take jobs ashore while the strike was on. You went into the union and they said it was a tactic to hold out longer, many of the lads were on the bones of their arse now and if you could get a start bloody well take it. And Cavanagh said the funds couldn't last forever even though they were only giving us three quid a week strike money; Eddy's cousin was a gangerman for Lloyds and had got him and Hayes a start and Eddy says do you want to give it a whirl, and you say dead right, and that Monday you were winding your way out of town and passing bits and pieces of the countryside and seeing old churches standing in the villages beyond Sefton and Ormskirk; and there was a hell of a difference between that and the quiet docks.

Each Friday you went down the union and signed the register and put your strike pay in the contributions box, and you heard a lot of the lads did the same, and the bloke behind the desk asked how it was going and you said not too bad, and then you'd take your board and stand on the docks for the day. Come the Monday you'd be in the country again and change your board for a spade, and the days passed slow and the sun shone and dinner times you'd sit and play cards in the hut or boot a ball about in massive football games on the back field, and the lads when they found out you were a seaman wanted to know all about it, and was it true what the papers were saying.

One pay day Eddy went around with a hat to take down to the union, and a couple of the moaners wouldn't put anything in, but the rest came good and there were a few quid by the time you took it down. And the union was fair pleased, and you knew they were bloody organised the way they'd spread it about. And you'd go in for a pint before heading down the docks and maybe give some of the others a drink, and many a time you saw Eddy slip a few bob and pay Nell something for the good turns. Those days were fine with something in your pocket and a bit of time at home, and you didn't mind the sites too much and when the moaners started on about holding the country to ransom you just told them to stuff it.

Down on the docks one time a gang of engineers passed you, and it must have been the chief or the second said something because all the others laughed, not real somehow but kind of sniggering, the way crawlers always laugh with their hands up by their faces. And Eddy shouted something back about them being sorry one day and gave them a mouthful, and the big fellow came over and said we'd never sail on their company, and Eddy said you'd have no bloody company without us, and a smile came over the big one's face and he said "we'll see, we'll see," and Eddy shouted it was hard luck on his mother as he walked away.

And the feeling was strong through those June days. Hardly any ships were docking now and there were hundreds more strung up side by side along the quays. And you thought they couldn't go anywhere without us. And the days passed by and the sun poured down, and you were one of the lucky ones going home and having a hot tea every night and a few drinks with your mates, and then on Fridays putting your good clothes on and strolling down to the union and clacking the paper against your leg onto the docks. And even the lads that weren't working, cheesed off and sick of it, you could see they weren't going to give way to those bastards on the 'pool'* either.

And the feeling stayed with you each time you walked down the stones and passed the quiet offices and the ships hovering above you, idle in the dock as much like iron ghosts with no men to work them, and passed the clutches of lads on

* The Merchant Navy Shipping Establishment, home of the Federation of ship owners has always been referred to as the pool. It is from there that ships are allocated to seamen.

the gates; no creak of winches or derricks swinging to and fro to disturb the sun on the water, or pull out cargo for the long sheds with their tarped roofs peeling in the heat.

And you rode in the works bus each morning and watched as the town gave way to the fields and the villages and the kids playing; kids that spoke in funny ooh aye accents, and you sat there and rolled your smoke and watched. And one day in late June you opened your paper and there on the banners ran the line 'Communists and Seamen', and underneath was what Wilson had said about a tightly knit group of politically motivated men playing with the country's fortune for their own ends. And you asked Eddy what the hell was going on and he shook his head and shrugged, and Cavanagh said it was a load of shit but he said that about everything.

And you got to work and everyone was talking about it, the moaners were going a mile a minute every break, and even the good lads weren't speaking up. And the crawlers laughed about whip rounds just to support the commies and who wanted to have them buggers here; all they wanted was to wreck the country, holding their bloody meetings and screaming and bawling for all the workers to join together and all that nonsense when there'd be no work for any of us; and all day it was communist this and communist that. You looked over the hut and Eddy had his face stuck in a newspaper and he still told them to get stuffed but his voice wasn't so big, so Cavanagh gets up and shouts the creeps down and Eddy looks up and laughs, then one of the creeps turns quick and says why doesn't he go back to bloody Russia and there's damn near a fight, and the ganger comes in and even if he's Eddy's cousin he's not looking too pleased. And its strange the way everything was all right up until Wilson made his comments.

And it's the same on the picket lines; people are shouting down at you from buses and you couldn't remember that before. And you swear you see and hear that bloody word communism more times in the next few days than you've ever done in your life. They've told Eddy to get back to Russia like he was a bloody tink himself: now they're on about it in the workshops and on the docks, and it makes you wonder with Nelly giving you a drink now and then and a free bus ride off the lads if you're not all bloody communists.

You went down to the pub that last Friday and saw Joe Conlan and a couple of others. Eddy had his back to you but you could tell by the way his head was bobbing up and down he was all tensed up about something. Joe had that same crooked smile running down his face the way you see in people who never believe in anything, and you heard him say they're all the same, the politicians, the union, the bloody lot of them. And there was Eddy shaking his head, bringing it backwards and forwards and scratching it, and saying what about these communists then, when Conlan picks up his mug and starts slowly to talk about Wilson and his boys and how with time passing for the government and bankers up in arms he'll do anything to get us back, and wouldn't care what sort of shit he threw. Joe looked up into Eddy's eyes and shook his head; you don't have to be in this game all your life to know that.

And it was the same on the Sunday with the papers full of it, and one even had a special couple of pages devoted to the strike with little pictures of the executive lined up side by side the way they photograph convicts, and showed the ones who were supposed to be communists. There were even pictures of Secretary Hogarth, but he wasn't saying anything, the bastard, and a couple of lads said he wanted us back after that Pearson report. And all that week Hogarth is on the telly and the wireless and you can see he isn't scared any more, and everyone is nice and respectable to him and look like they even feel sorry for him, having to deal with those other buggers in the union.

Then you were humping timber and having the joists laid out ready for the carpenters, when one of the moaners passes by and he's laughing and makes a sign like to pick up your cards, and shouts over that the strike has been called off. And you find the others and take an early bus home to catch the news, and your old lady gives Eddy a drink of tea and your old man is sat in the chair, and Hogarth comes on and he's looking serious with his little face and eyes peering over his glasses and a faint Scottish accent, and says the executive have taken a decision to end the dispute. And no-one asks him what made the seamen change their minds so suddenly, before the General Secretary drones on about the Prime Minister's speech and how talk of communism didn't affect the executive's decision, and your old man starts to laugh. And you don't know what to think, and sit looking at the bastard and wonder about all the good lads that have watched the days and weeks go by with fluff in their pockets, and you look over at Eddy and he says nothing. Then your old man mutters that they're all the bloody same anyway.

So you went back and it was as simple as that. It had all happened so fast. You went down the union the next morning still not knowing what was going on, and it didn't look like many others knew either, when you heard there was going to be a meeting down on the pier head. And you walked down the stones and saw the warehouses and the workshops all getting ready for the return, and a queue of wagons stretched the length of the dock road. Skippers and mates were flooding back to the ships in taxis, and suddenly you thought of Ronnie Ferguson's house, and you thought of a few other things as you carried on down.

And it wasn't the same feller that you'd seen that time with Billy Cook, laughing and talking and shaking hands down on the gates. He was quieter and his face looked under strain, and he was telling you to go back lads, the union had decided. And Billy was now saying we'd always been solid and how our strike committee had been one of the best, and the lads up there with him gave a few sad little smiles, but we all had to go back now. He knew we hadn't got all we came out for but no-one was going to have to work nearly sixty hours a week any more, and there was this Pearson report. And you remembered it was this same feller said the report wasn't worth a bag of crisps only a little while back, and he'd let Wilson know when the union went to Downing Street. And even as he was telling you to return you knew he didn't mean it. He was only doing what

Hogarth and those other bastards up there in London were telling him, and Conlan's words came rushing back and you thought this bloke was just another one of them, but listening to the unsure ring of his words you didn't really believe that. He was only a feller doing what he could.

And oh, they were as nice as pie to you down on the 'pool': mister this and mister that and would you like to come this way, and you knew that would change soon enough when they'd all their ships away. And you felt lousy as you rode down on the bus with Eddy and Cavanagh to the Harrison yards and you thought, forget it you'll be sailing out before the end of the week, and so you tried not to bother.

Then that night after you'd signed on you went down the pub and drank pint after pint, and Eddy started on again about his freedom and Hayes told him to give it a miss, it was all over now wasn't it. And you bought more and more drink, and took a taxi up to Nelly Flanagan's and gave her a few for all the good turns, and woman that she was she bought a few back off the top shelf, and the rum and the whisky was going down. Then Nelly closed up and drew the curtains and you drank some more, until there were only shillings left from the advance notes; and you were whirling down past the docks and even at this time ships were moving out through the locks, and you could see the lights and hear the tugs on the water and you fell laughing up the gang plank, and a mate looked down from the bridge and gave a sad little smile. And Hayes hammered his feet against the deck and roared up into the night and kicked a cardboard box that went spinning through the air and landed on water below, the black water unruffled by any ships' passage these last six weeks.

And on the deck the middle of the morning, the sun prinking on the water and glistening on the winches and twine and loading booms, and the mates nice as pie and you standing there and not doing much and no-one seeming to care; the engineers coming up from below tell you how much they'd enjoyed the rest and the subsistence money and had we had a nice holiday, and they stop smiling when they see Eddy's face.

Then the third mate comes up and tells you a bit curt to do something, and the chief sees him and weaves down the companionway and pulls him to one side, and you can see he's putting a fly in his ear. The dockers are just coming back from their tea and there's a few lads hanging around the galley to see what's on for the dinner, and the winches haven't started up yet and suddenly there's a moment of great quietness on the dock, with the ships resting in the haze and a faint drone of sound from the city, and the smell of tarpaulin and oil in the air.

And you hear Eddy's voice mumbling something and grow louder, and you look up and see him there with the hair falling down his face, and he flings aside his painting rag and puts his hand up to his head and your mind goes racing back to the time when he sang the 'Saints' out on the deck so long ago. And he's cursing the mates and the engineers and the owners and every bastard, on again about freedom and wasted lives and what it's doing to us; and a couple of the lads start smiling and this sets him off worse, and you stand there looking at him and feel his eyes on you calling you up, and you think of all the times you've spent together, the drinking and the laughter and the waiting down on the docks, the work and the whip-rounds and poor Sid Fletcher and then the union's sad voice telling us to go back.

Well we are back; back in the same old game and sailing out on the night tide, and it rises up inside you until you feel you're going to choke, and Eddy's working his tongue around communism and roaring it out till it rings down the stones, and people are looking now. The moment of quietness has passed and Eddy stands within it, his hands balled up and the words, torrents of them, floating down the docks and people aren't laughing any more, and the bosun comes up to get a grip of him but he's having none of it. Then suddenly you're with him and the pair of you are shouting and carrying on, and you can see the skipper peering down from the bridge, and you don't care because no bastards can sail the ships without us, and you stand there and curse and shout communist right back in their

70

faces and watch them blink; and it's a sunny morning in Liverpool and the strike is finished, but the voice is yours and you know things can never be the same, and when you've said your piece the two of you make a smoke and go back to work and no-one says a word, and Joe Conlan looks over and smiles that smile of his, and shakes his head as if you'll never learn.

UNEASY MOMENTS AT SEVEN SISTERS

I was working as the boss that day. The others could do nothing with Carmel so they sent her to me. Counselling was taking place all over that floor. Every cubicle was filled. Rubber plants and smouldering ash trays separated the light.

Carmel came in, her handkerchief delicately held, the fine lines of her face etched with fatigue and bad nights. On the telephone her training manager told it all. The word processing course had turned sour, office practice into cures for anorexia, filing and reception duties into a disquisition on men's legs behind the heavy sliding metal. No-one knew why she was coming back. The manager had terminated her. Her dole was in question.

I looked at her severely. She was going to feel the power. I focused the chair and brought up my glasses higher with the authoritarian finger. Her handkerchief clenched, the tears rolled then flowed. Hard talk fell into sobs, a strand of her hair became loose. Defensive. The manager was lying, the course leader mistaken. She had not absented willingly. The tutor was a degenerate, dumb to his charges, but no, oh no, not to her. She turned her head in disgust.

Sunlight flared, I softened. I could see the patterns in the tweed of her skirt. Could she see my shape amidst the dust beams? Everything was going to be smoothed. Soothingly I spoke and spoke until my voice made no sense to me. The word processing course was again available. Office practice would again come on stream. Carmel had only to phone. The college was arranged, the tutor to be interviewed

Her eyes lit up and sparkled. She hid a laugh behind her forty eight beaten summers. She clutched her handbag and spoke of Ireland. Her face became coquettish. What were her chances of becoming a beautician? My eyes felt suddenly tired. The pain crept up slowly from the back of the head. I coughed. The madness always started like this. Head waiters who turn gangster suddenly want to become engineers, electronics experts. Those with provisional licenses see themselves behind the wheels of 40 tonners. Hands which have hardly held a brush are convinced marbling, stippling and graining is for them. Would be plumbers who never smelled a sewer are queuing at my door.

Carmel looked at her nails. She talked of fulfilment. Office work was alienating. The last word picked up speed like a pinball and went cascading through my mind. What was wrong with wanting nice clothes and cars and sympathetic people. A sympathetic man; there was always America. If only she could get some sleep.

They were fighting seven to a bed in the council bedsit above her. Bumps and cries and crashes all night long. Africans, African music. It made Carmel despair. Her face looked as if she had seen some time upstairs. I coughed again and she sighed. We were back to the Office Course. The best I could do. It was getting hot. Sweat streaked her forehead. Sunbeams crept over the dusty veneer of the desk. I could feel the dampness under the armpits. An anguished cry came up from the corridor. The first that day but not the last from our cubicles. The interview was over. She smiled and rose. Her head full of appointments and my succour. Piety had its place.

Another success, another repentant drawing up dreams like leaden skirts into the life of work and unwork. They were queuing up outside. Too many, always too many at the dream factory. Milling around the secretary's desk, Black faces, Chinese and White faces, Asian ladies in saris and coats, dogs, babies, saddened Jews and Poles and Turks. It was like the death ship. Except we were all aboard the Government's training plan.

And meanwhile stretched flat on a bed in a darkened room, on the outskirts of town, Ephrem Hertzenburg lay with the cancer eating him and morphine at his side.

All the papers devoted special pages to his death, which had been expected for some days. Students and others who had passed that stage had full length photographs of him in their minds. They lost this picture with the newspaper's printed image. Psychoanalysts were sad and relieved when he died. When he was stirred up he did things many of them would never imagine doing even on their best days.

After the ceremony there was much talk of synthesis and existentialism. Everyone went to the cafes afterwards, and the pictures and obituaries from that day's paper were folded up and put away in pockets to fade like the sunlight in our office.

Carmel walked up the hill and saw the hearse and the disappearing cars. She smiled. It was sad, but she would never be that way. No way. Her beauty stalked the world.

GREY DAWN BREAKING

Tony Lane's book takes its title from the last line of the famous stanza of John Masefields poem, you know the one, "I must go down to the sea again, to the lonely sea and sky." But it is the seamen themselves who are lonely these days. It is a loneliness without ships.

The once seething waterside life of the great ports is now a thing of the past, containing all the more hurt because of such recent associations. From the war until the mid seventies, two weeks without a ship and you began to worry - now it is a year or more. Sitting in a dockside bar with the hotels and car parks for company, with all the images of Theme Park Britain rising up before you, the talk doesn't lend itself other than to cynics or sardonic laughter, "Go away to sea, young man."

But you can't rub out the memories, and this is the strength of the book, of how even the most recent past keeps dancing in the present. Based largely on the experiences of the post-war seamen and more particularly in the period between 1950-1980, it illustrates, long after the music has finished, the myriad complexities, the self denial and self mockery, the working of ships from the metropolis to the far flung peripheries. Descriptions of the weather, the companionship, the isolation are all contained here but shining through them, the different components of the class and ethnic structures of ships as a microcosm of the society from which they came.

If for many seamen, Officers and ratings alike - and there were almost 200,000 of them in 1955 - the decline in their numbers to only a fraction of that former figure is not only due to changes in technology but a refusal on the part of the British Government to subsidise the British Fleet, then the consequences, like the philosophy, lies at the heart of changed routes and patterns of trade. It is here that the decline of Empire has its last laugh, and brings to the fore all the divisions and sub divisions that marked life aboard ship between middle class deck officers, skilled workers in officers uniforms like the engineers, and then the great welter of "ratings" brought up on such sayings as "oil and water don't mix", and "all stewards are arses", and not surprisingly divided between deck, engine and catering. Bring into the picture the West African seamen, the Arabs, the Lascars and Chinese to service the white officer command of ships, and we have some idea of how seamen acted as symbols of a particular society with its base in an Empire culture. The loss of a merchant fleet is the breaking of those connections.

And yet it is only in the last ten years that the full consequences have dawned. "Just thirty years ago....the world's ports were full of red ensigns. Imperial dependencies upon which the (Shipping) industry had grown and prospered were still strong. The British people were pleased to be able to convince themselves that they still had an Empire by calling it a Commonwealth, and self delusion was particularly easy for seamen."

From being standard bearers of the Empire under the tutelage of an authoritarian dictatorial and racist union, seamen gather in the dockside bars that have remained and show two fingers to the world for the way they have been treated. In more sedate ways, so too the officers from their suburbs. It is an irony that the National Union of Seamen has become stronger, more democratic and progressive, just as the numbers of seamen have declined.

Yet complex as they are, these questions form the historical and sociological boundaries of the book. What beats at the very heart is the attempt to capture the everyday life of seafaring, seen and experienced from every different point in the hierarchy of the ship. The trick is not letting the big questions intrude, and if they are never very far from the surface, the skill is not only in the construction of the weaving of a story, but in the way the reader must evaluate different settings that often appear to contradict at one level, then harmonise at another.

They are posed, often more subtly than the easy generalisations of corporatism or of an industry that sees itself as a "service"; from the chuntering of the Daily Telegraph during the Falklands "crusade" that the fleet was the fourth arm of the State, to a communist bosun's perception of his post-war experience, the book has a great feel for the "heightened moments" of shipboard life. Two quotes from the text may help to illustrate this point .

"When it came to introductions into the world of work, Billy Kerrigan's mother had her dead husband's discharge books bound together with an elastic band; Len Holder had the Glenn Line's choice pilot...... When ten middle class boys end up as senior officers and ten working class boys end up as bosuns and cooks, it is reasonable to suppose that individual will and choice have little to do with the outcome."

Compare this however, to a passage in the same chapter, and we have instances of the overall totality of going away. " For those seafarers, though they will not talk voluntarily of it, there is still the exaltation of a tropical night, a spectacular landfall at sunrise. There is the companionability when chance sets up a crew and master who like and respect each other; there is escape from the madness of the headline: there is the clean simplicity of butting into a headwind hurtling out of a white whiskered blue sky. There is the going ashore in a strange and exotic place when for once luck runs your way. These are, all of them, idealisations of moments cut free from the repetitious routine of work and social relationships. But here aboard ship, as everywhere else, it is the compensations that define the life."

This is a great book for anyone interested in the sea and the lives of those who have been formed around it. As an ethnographic study it is a way of reading labour history beyond the confines of the institutions, yet caught in the social web of the ship itself which, even more than the small, intense world of the dockside, has so bedevilled any one single union or explanation. The outcome is a contribution to a labour culture which memory only might refresh, but which nevertheless illustrates and helps pattern the present disaster.

Those idealisation of moments bear other resonance now - perhaps the real tragedy is the young working class will no longer see the funnels of the Harrisons or the "Bluey's" and dream of getting out, if only for a while, but they have informed generations of people in a traditional sea going city like Liverpool and other port towns.

Yet seamen themselves, who are well aware of this and know the prices paid, will recognise in this chronicle another voice that has been away and later returned to swagger along the stones. Whether in self mockery or pride is not really the point; there was no lonely sea and sky then, even if time was temporary.

British Merchant Seafarers in the late 20th Century.
Manchester University Press, 1986.
By Tony Lane.

CONRAD'S LETTERS

Here is Conrad writing from his adopted home in Kent, while London "lay threatening" half a day's travel away across the Thames. Conrad had finally given up the sea after more than twenty years as mate and master on British merchant ships. This period finds him agonising not only about his acceptability to the British literati - he had been disowned by Polish intellectuals for abandoning name, language, and nation - but of the problems and sense of order imperialism brought to his own work.

Worries pervade this collection of letters. Even with the success of the Nigger of the Narcissus (1898), working towards the completion of Heart of Darkness (1899) and Lord Jim (1900), doubts rear up in him at every turn. Conrad's own work and the structure of the society he lived in, often fill him with dread. Perhaps that is what makes them so interesting - the editors are to be congratulated here for a fine production, helpful comments and bibliographical notes throughout. What they do not illustrate is the tension, the desire within Conrad for a sense of place and recognition of his art, in contrast to the certainties of the British upper- and middle-classes. Yet outwardly, these were precisely the characteristics that Conrad appeared to share. It is this paradox that illuminates these letters.

Writing to Edward Lancelot "Ted" Sanderson, an ardent imperialist, at the declaration of the Boer War in 1899, Conrad was to mention that,

"The danger to the Empire is not in South Africa, but is everlastingly skulking in the Far East."

Yet drawing analogies between the order, discipline and illusions of Empire with his own work, he continued:

"If you knew how ambitious I am, how my ambition checks my pen at every turn. Doubts assail me from every side. The doubt of form - the doubt of tendency - a mistrust of my own conceptions - and scruples of the modern order. Ridiculous, isn't it? As if my soul mattered to the Universe.

But even as the ant bringing its grain of sand to the modern edifice, may justly think itself important, so I would like to think I am doing my appointed work."

If the Nigger of the Narcissus was in Conrad's words, "to do the highest kind of justice to the physical universe," then there was often a tendency within himself to portray his characters as belonging firmly within an established social order. If they had none of this sense of station they were lost. Mere flotsam and jetsam if they were ordinary sailors, irretrievable angst if they were something higher in social standing.

It was Conrad's sense of social hierarchy that the communist seaman, George Garrett, identified in an essay in the magazine The Adelphi in 1936. He took exception to the way the seaman Donkin had been portrayed as the malingerer and dirty rebel who would ultimately be responsible for the decline of the Empire. Conrad, he suggested, had bumped up against "some of these Liverpool hard cases", and wrote out his prejudice in the Nigger of the Narcissus in the form of a conservative-minded ship's officer, where his art and his social views intermingled as one.

Conrad's Donkin:

"Looked as if he had been cuffed....kicked....rolled in the mud. He had knocked about for a fortnight ashore in the native quarter, 'Bombay', cadging for drinks, starving, sleeping on rubbish heaps. This clean, white forecastle was his refuge, where he could be lazy and curse the food he ate. This unsympathetic and undeserving creature, that knows all about his rights but knows nothing of the courage, endurance, of the unexpressed faith and unspoken loyalty that knits together a ship's company."

This view of the social hierarchy confirmed Conrad's prejudice towards the lower decks. For Garrett, the Donkins of this world would "one day write the real story of the sea" as it existed on the water line.

For Conrad, it was always as the gentleman and authoritarian that won the battle for everyday living, his review of

Hugh Clifford's essays, Studies in Brown Humanity (1898) were to echo this code of Empire. Clifford, a colonial administrator in Malaya, published many stories and sketches of life on the Peninsular, admiring the customs and ways of the natives. Conrad wrote sombrely in The Academy of April 1898:

"One cannot expect to be at the same time a ruler of men and an irreproachable player on the flute."

It was the moral and fate of Empire and those whose lives rested within it, that were never far from Conrad's thoughts in the writing of Heart of Darkness and Lord Jim. To the poet and critic, W. E. Henley, who was to publish the Nigger of the Narcissus in serial form in the New Review, he thanked the good fortune that kept him afloat in the temporary seas of uncertainty after 1898, the last time he applied for command of a ship.

Conrad wrote,

"A chance comes once in life to all of us. Not the chance to get on, that only comes to good men. Fate is inexorably just. But Fate is also merciful and even to the poorest there comes sometimes the chance of an intimate, complete and pure satisfaction. That chance comes to me when you accepted the Nigger. I have got it. I hold it, I keep it and all the machinations of my private devils cannot rob me of it."

His letters to the Scottish aristocrat and socialist, Hugh Cunninghame-Graham, reflect this ontological despair.

"International fraternity may be an object to strive for and in sober truth, since it has your support, I will try to think it serious, but.....there is already as much fraternity as there can be and that is very little and that very little is no good." (He continues in French, translated by the editors within the text). "Man is a vicious animal. His viciousness must be organised. Society is fundamentally criminal or it would not exist. Selfishness preserves everything we love and everything we hate, and everything holds together - for myself I look at the future from the depths of a very dark past and I find I am allowed fidelity to an absolutely lost cause, to an idea without a future (only truth remains, a sinister and fleeting ghost whose image is impossible to fix). Towards myself I practise a fierce and rational selfishness, therein I pause. Then thinking returns. Life starts again, regrets, memories, and a hopelessness darker than night."

This is the world of Heart of Darkness and Lord Jim. If he had a sneaking regard for "The most extreme anarchist", who wanted to obliterate all structures of society, and whom he was to write about later in The Secret Agent; Conrad also perceived the Empire, the city of London as its financial centre was like every ship's company, a a hierarchical site of power. But one that had to be continued with if only for a sense of propriety.

He would have recognised George Orwell's words, written nearly 30 years later in Burmese Days (1928) as an officer required to kill an elephant. An action he was loath to commit, but if he did not, then: "The crowd would laugh at me. And my whole life, every white man's life in the East, was one long struggle not to be laughed at."

Conrad's hesitations about his own work - such a concern in the period 1898-1900 - are brushed away by the end of this collection of letters, as if he is now convinced of the validity of his vision. In 1902 he is writing to William Blackwood, the publisher, and announcing:

"My work shall not be an utter failure...because it has the solid base of a definite intention - first. And next, because it is not an endless analysis of affected sentiments but in its essence it is action (strange as this affirmation may sound at the present time). Nothing but action, action observed, felt and interpreted, with an absolute truth to my sensations (which are the basis of art and literature). Action of human beings that will bleed to a prick, and are moving in a visible world...this is my creed. Time will show.''

This is the view from Conrad, the established writer, at home in Kent while the City of London lay, not now so menacing, across the Thames; whose art was a fleeting series of images, moulded by his imagination, and experience along the trading routes of the Empire; but ultimately it was always an art as viewed from the bridge. These letters provide an interesting illustration of Conrad's internal voyaging at the high-water mark of British Imperialism, where every runnel and gutter was awash with human jetsam.

The Collected Letters of Joseph Conrad, Volume II, 1898-1902.
Edited by F.R.Karl and Laurence Davids,
Cambridge University Press, 1986

LOOSE CHANGE

The lines of the horses were drawn tight across the entrance. The wind would now and then rise and flap the capes of the cops sat astride them facing the crowd. Behind them, visors shining, the riot police were bunched into a glittering fist, and after them came the Mets, whose temper was well known. The streets around the plant were black and shot with wind; electric light oozed from the houses where the inhabitants had stayed up for the spectacle.

The charge began, the screams and shouts. The television was there with flashes of cameras and soundmen hanging from the walls. Sunday entertainment for the silent majority. A Union is dying on the line and Wapping, where the wind bends and blows from the river, is being woven into the fabric of the rubbish press and the national life, and it's all being run by foreigners anyway, that's the beef, as the crowds are chanting "peaceful" under the clubs and foaming horses.

Seething with injustice, I sit within the dark club. Only a month ago you could sit all night and pay only for your beer, but Manolo has got married. His wife is a bitch. She's English. Now there is a cover charge of a couple of quid, the beer has gone up, the food too. West End. They are going higher in the market. When he dances now it doesn't have the same pleasure. She watches everything like a hawk, the bitch.

The Flamenco begins, the dancer in her red dress arches hands above head, she twirls, her heels stamp the wooden floor. Behind me is the glass jar with the entrance money. They have taken the notes away, but the sovereigns are heaped in a little pile. The guitar twangs, the lights are down, a voice wails of the South and all eyes are for the twirling dancer. I reach behind me quick and empty the glass, meaning only to take the entrance money, but too late. The song has finished. The glass is empty, my fist bulges with sovereigns. The woman is standing above me, English as sin.

"It's hospital food for you" she says, and draws up a couple of butchers. They push me into the alley with the bins and

84

cardboard boxes, and one smashes me in the gob. They are starting to work a nice rhythm with me when Manolo comes down. He was sweating. He helped me to my feet. Some blood went onto his jacket. He helped me to the street and gave me back some money. He wasn't a bad guy, his old man was better but his wife was a bitch. I told him. He said "Don't bother me;" another time like this and it would be curtains. Wapping talk.

I walked up to the "Blue Posts" and sat on the steps. Someone gave me a cigarette. If you have a good coat on and are going bald, and are sat bleeding in the doorway of a pub in early morning Soho, they think you're in the transition between bohemianism and a bum. That's why a lot of them try to get their act together in the later part of the evening, they can go to hell after that. Patriotism would only be a kick up the arse before eleven.

I was looking rough at the best time and they gave me cigarettes, someone pressed money in my hand. I held out my other and more came in. Life was wonderful at this hour of the morning. People weren't scared or shut in; someone was talking about daffodils and blowing gardens and all night vigils. All this on the blues of that city street, I ask you. I could have cried with him, long raking tears into the night. Maybe communism is only some peace of mind, a communion well away from Church and State. Whatever it is, you can be sure the shit starts when the secret gets out, or when the dream turns real. The Empire was supposed to be our communion.

Everywhere you look they accuse you of treason. It is no longer a cause for laughing. Yet laugh we did as seamen, laughed throughout time, especially when the Empire was threatened. We knew what it was built on. Company spies and spies for the Nation, the jewel of the working class, our Union in the 1920s. Oh yes, they were up to their necks highlighting our patriotism. When there was a strike blame the commos for usurping the common seaman. And the 1930s the same, all blamed on the men "whose bad influence was gotten in the Southern Irish ports". All under the influence of that other spy, De Valera and his misbegotten Republic.

Even in the 1940s when Billy Hart and Pat Murphy stopped the Queen Mary, it was the work of knaves, determined to undermine the country, "when Church and State are working for the reconstruction of the land." And all the time it was patriots telling you this; Union leaders, Ship owners, Captains, Politicians. In the 1950s it was "experienced agitators" after a strike over the strumming of guitars, and in 1960, Elder Dempsters had men on their payroll to deal with subversion, like the old Cunard spies. All reports made their way to IRIS, that think tank of Patriotism whose offices were housed under the same roof as the Seaman's Union. Spies and agitators all of them.

Labour Prime Ministers, like Wilson whose grandad ran the workhouse, who poured wrath on Communism within the union, "on men who show no liking nor respect for the democratic processes of this country", when the bankers tugged his tail. Fifty years of spying and fear and paranoia have left their mark. Even those once on the left, now recount to TUC conferences about the ways they were encouraged. A whiff of patriotism is in the air, always the same when the mood turns nasty. The search for a power base, the launch of a crusade.

And Seamen have been the object of crusades throughout history, whose bread has forever had seven crusts. I sit there and smoke on the Tottenham Court Road and hold out my hands to show a man of peace, with battered face, continuing to live. Another gust of people sweep by; peals of laughter as offerings to the night, the money drops onto my nails, my caulked bulwarks, my riveted plates, my empty seaports, my fleet that is dying.

The night was aching with love, those uncertain fields through which so many aliens have danced. I too set on my way across Oxford Street and down to Leicester Square through the seething late night crowds. Teeth and faces swam before me. On the corner of Charing Cross Road a taxi pulled close, and awaited the lights. Roars and laughter came from inside, faces pressed to the glass and to the night. They recognised a seaman these Scandinavians, even one without a ship. There were women in there with them. The driver was not happy when I opened the door, but he knew there was money. He tipped his shades back onto his face when they shouted for more. A young women gave me a handkerchief, a bottle was produced. We were sailing down the wide boulevards of the State. The young woman was from Germany, her friends were being rubbed by the seamen. I took a long drink; she came and sat next to me on the folding seats.

We got out on the Battersea Bridge, the taxi went clattering on its way, the long way around to Rotherhithe. Apart from the docks at Tilbury, only a few wharves were being worked on the river. Convoys wharf I knew of old, when the water seethed with shipping around the Isle of Dogs. We looked down from the bridge at the dark water rolling east. The print would be next; everyone knew it, but you still had to fight. The lights from the embankment bounced on the water. The seamen had given me money. There had been no tap. They had more than enough, and could not be bothered at this ashes time of the morning. Anyway, they had something more than money, they had women with them in a cold and foreign land.

We bought hamburgers and sat with the bike gangs on the bridge. There were hundreds of them, getting stored up before they burned down Kent. They had women, booze and drugs with them all ready for a show piece. Before that, terrified citizens would wake, sweating in their beds as they roared through villages and market towns on the way to the coast. They were sat astride or fingering each others bikes now, swearing, testing, wiping with greasy rags the creatures that stood blue and crimson and gold.

We stood amongst them and they eyed us up and down, wondering about my cut face and bald dome, and the young girl. Their women blew smoke rings around their chains and tossed their heads. Behind them the caravan stall was heaving with orders, onions swam across the counter in seas of tomato sauce, the generator was bumbling like a fairground in full swing, and the whole place shone like a jewel in the night. We stumbled across the road and hitched up over the railings into the park. They couldn't work out what she was doing with an old fuck like me. A tired cheer went up as they watched us climb over. They too were enemies.

When we came back they were well gone. The caravan was shuttered and bolted, and the first light was up in the sky. We walked over to the Embankment and up along the river. A cold spring green stubbled the blackness of the trees. The Nazis had taken her grandfather for being in with the union. Her old man was still in shock in that green lit 1950s Germany, with Konrad Adenauer and the divided state. What a time for patriots. She was born in the middle 1960s, the last in a long line that threaded German history; when Cable Street was still Cablestrasse, and cafe society had its own way of doing things in Stepney and Poplar and Bethnal Green. Born at the time of the great strike, when seamen marched with placards that said "remember 1911" in memorials of the surge of syndicalism that saw the consolidation of the union, born in the post-war boom. We walked through Parliament Square, and up past the Reform Club towards Tower Bridge. I wanted to go back to Wapping to watch the scabs come out.

We wanted a glimpse of the silent majority whose houses in the suburbs meant more than anything. People who hid behind closed curtains in their protected coaches. People who drank Perrier water and ran Volvos if they had their chance. The economy and the nation; imports cost jobs, but who gave a fuck when you had extra money for strike breaking. Ask the police, they know better than anyone. Seamen were always told that if the Empire folded there would be no jobs for anyone. Someone quoted Hillaire Belloc at the 1963 conference, about drinking from empty cups when the ships stopped coming. It was always the company men that took heed; most of the others had to have something to kick against just to survive. Their patriotic bosses changed the colour of the flag when it came to money, heroes of popular capitalism, take your choice, they amount to the same. But don't talk to me about patriots or spies.

She walks alongside me, whistling, kicking stones, looking at the water. She could be my grand-daughter if I had one. I could use a smoke. No more sitting on the pavement now, this wasn't Soho. It was a different time of day. People everywhere were stirring with their fears. Insecurities were being brought out like icons, being rubbed down, paranoias burnished like brass. All that was cast aside in the nights' festivities now returned like ashes to the throat. Fear gleams like diamonds on the rings of the women. Men finger their pyjamas and wish they were in Brazil. And we are coming from up river after passing the night on pavements and bridges and park shelters, shambling along like Gorky's animals of Odessa to our own particular Bethlehem, where someone will give us a smoke as we stand on the line, and sooner or later a cup of coffee will change hands.

Manolo's old man made good coffee. And always had plenty to go with it. They called him a spy and a communist. Well, Franco did. He was lucky. He got out on the MacAndrews boats and did not ever go ashore again through the olives or the orange groves, nor even touch the dockside walls of the church at Valencia. A good bloke. We used to have a drink around here when he worked on the shore gang. Later, he brought his family and they lived in Whitechapel. Young Manolete runs the clubs now, but he's getting fat and married a bitch and settled for the suburbs. He doesn't bother, not like his dad, twirling and fighting to the end. Twirling and fighting like a firework, defending his corner where no ships come anymore and no seamen walk the streets. The print was always a refuge, a haven, and now that harbour is being destroyed. It was the old game, they clear away the unions and they create more spies with the changing winds.

Wapping, in the cold blowing morning with ragged black clouds and rain on the way, two streets down from Cable Street where Fascism was defeated, and not just by the English. Who's laughing now, bastards. They come out in their shuttered coaches and the cries go up. And me, roaring at them; an old man and a girl whose father was born in pre-war Germany.

That doesn't mean I like her the less. And she likes me, an old fuck who can feel the blood rising just the same. And shouts out on the line, stop the bastards, the fucking bastard slags. And even the inhabitants of this waterside look a bit disjointed when they see him, bumps all over his face and a trickle of blood from one of Manolo's heavies, struggling and shouting. No love for the filth or the scabs down here, but you can feel the looks, and with the young girl; strange. That whore in Manolo's club, watching everything like a hawk, even she would know. "Its hospital food for you, O'Brien."

Seething with injustice, we stand here in the dawn amidst the strewn bricks, the broken glass glittering the road where the police had come with painted faces and no numbers. The flats are quiet now. The spectacle is over. The Nation State dances like a leg severed from the torso they once called Empire. And those who cannot sing the song are spies. Enemies from within. Allusions the seamen have grown old with or laughed at, or occasionally risen against in fury. I put my tongue in the young girls mouth. She can taste my resurrection.

WE GET LOST

If I can call you baby
And others call you dear
What does it matter sweetheart
When strangers meet like ships
And sounds are blurred
In the fog of love.

When hopes are born
And are named by rivers.
In slurry heaps of Blankets
The engine room of Mattresses
On coaxed pillows,
Siren songs
For love baby, love.

C'mon sweet lover unfurl
your thighs and sheets
billowing like topsails
We chart the gloaming
naked in the spangled light
to those places. Without name.

CAST

A man and a woman slipped out from the little culvert where they had parked the car. They could hear the sound of the sea coming from behind the houses which the drizzling rain had stitched together in clusters along the front; everywhere lay calm as lunchtime settled over the village. Small children with older men for protection hurried to the closing shops for pies and sandwiches to go with their midday drink. The couple drifted along. It was the first day of their holiday after the long drive from Liverpool, where a love of the sea and the industrial villages of this Northumbrian coast had brought them.

Miners, with the blue scars of their existence etched into their hands and faces passed them by, packets of cigarettes bulged the pockets of their sportshirts beneath their lightweight macs. The man indicated, and she smiled in response and noted them cross the empty road into the pub, situated next to the ugly blackwalled chapel and the social club where the lunchtime bingo was in session.

The man and the woman were hungry, and stopped outside a cafe to see if it had fish. They always ate fish when they were on the coast. The cafe Riviera down the road sold only hamburgers. Of the village's two fish and chip shops one had closed for lunch, and the other had departed for holidays even though it was August. Tourism was no great attraction here. This cafe sold haddock and chips. Looking around, they said they would come back, faintly irritated by this lack of choice.

They turned to walk to the sea. Older men stood gazing at the boats and the grey water topped with white caps, while children played at the edge with a ball, and a dog splashed and shook on the sand. A tractor pulled like a bird at the rolling ramps that were used to perch the fishing boats high up on the beach; revving its boxed engine, it took a hold, and drove both ramp and boat into the sea amidst a great flurry of spume and water bubbling and frothing around the wheels. The men then scrambled aboard.

The boats were painted crimson and cream, and blue and cream and stood like prows along the strip of sand until the tractor came for them; resting now on the water, they seemed to settle themselves and unfurl in the way swans do after being on the land. Plastic bivouacs were stretched as shelter from the forecastle to midships in case the wind blew up, and on aft the great wooden rudder was fitted firmly into place. The boats were called 'cobles' by the people around here and as they tacked into the wind the man suddenly turned and felt as lonely as he had ever done.

Looking towards the headland, the church stood like a sentinel to face the east, and across the bay the coal mines and dock yards of Blyth were dark on the waterside sketching the far horizon. For just that moment of his turning the woman loved the man completely, until she suppressed the sentiment with a yawn and watched him wait for the last boat to depart; the tractor alone now with only the water to bubble around the wheels, and an old man who parried the steering with deft hands away from where the fleet had struck.

"What are you thinking about ?" she asked, a bit cruel.

"Now then" he muttered, and caught her yawn.

The woman caught his affectation, and they both laughed in a muted exaggeration for a love that had passed. She watched workers drift along the street by the arcade, the betting shop, the cafe, accompanied by wives, parents and children and thought time would just go on up here, bleak and irrespective of existence. The thin strand of beach, the decaying church and the modern mine, all vying with time itself for survival.

"I remember " she began in a different voice, a voice almost to herself, and stopped. Somewhere from deep within her unhappiness suddenly welled up and nearly made her choke. She closed her eyes, and was back in another country where they had first met, stretching her arms out to a landscape that offered nothing but solitude, a solitude precious in its own silent form, a solitude stolen by him, and a beauty of sun and moon and slow turned earth where girls danced on wooden floors and wore flowers in their hair. "Before", what a simple word, before she had known him? Before the studies, the growth, the excitement of new territory, the life of the mind, of a class, before philosophy? God, what did it matter; but she felt deep within her something mattered

They turned away from the waterfront and silently walked back to the cafe. She sank down exhausted onto the hard chair and looked out at the rain. The street was empty outside, and they ordered fish when the woman came. "What were you thinking all that time?" He looked at her, and in a parody of his action she shook her head and saw again in his eyes that terrible look of frustration that had so penetrated her. He lifted his fork, glanced at the sound of a fly, and felt that the moment demanded some kind of gesture from him. He lit a cigarette, and blew smoke carefully upwards at the ceiling in the face of this inchoate feeling of rage.

The woman set two plates of fish and chips before them. He watched her walk away, young, almost girlish really, with braided hair and big thighs. He let a look of sex wander disarmingly across his face like a direction in a map. The woman across from him at the table turned away humiliated, and snapped over into anger.

"There's a girl who wouldn't want you." she said, her voice too high. Heads turned.

"Don't." he soothed, his voice the calm of triumphant restraint. The point was taken. He stubbed out his cigarette.

They took a fork full from the haddock lying before them on the plate, and chewed slowly in anticipation. The fish tasted like something squeezed from a tube of glue, yet under the stares of the women servers and the other families sat around them, they ate on. Perspiration rose in beads on his forehead as he tried to eat too quickly, and the ulcer flared within the bed of his stomach. He wiped his face and looked away from her, his eyes full of hate.

There is never an isolation so profound as over meal times with the disenchanted. Something slight, as casual as the slackening of the mouth, the stiffness of the head as it searches for accommodation, to convey what depths, what acknowledgement of absence two people can share together. She turned her eyes towards him somehow to help him from his misery, but he was as obdurate as her earlier moments, and they drank away the taste of the fish with strong tea and silence.

The minutes passed slowly, with only the rain and idle chatter to relieve the monotony, and then from the kitchen came the sound of a terrible coughing and an older woman appeared who had not been present earlier. She looked in charge.

"Did you enjoy your meal pets?" she called over.

He looked at her and across to his own partner, whose eyes were fixed on her plate as if inwardly trying to digest the mounds of heavy yellow batter she had discarded with the fish.

"Lovely thanks." his face creased in an attempt at a smile, and within it the woman looked up and nodded her agreement. She regarded the face of the woman who approached, and noted it carried a jaundiced colour on her high cheekbones; yellow as that batter wrapped around the fish she thought, and then chided herself for her cruelty.

"You're not well?" She asked with that innocent expression of directness that was such a part of her, and in which others could sometimes see a source of compassion.

"Am not pet, am not." the older one replied with equal candour.

There were circles framed around her eyes from lack of sleep, deep purple rings that struck into her and gave evidence of an emptiness that was as hard to find as it was to explore. She was returning for more radiotherapy in the coming weeks. As she gathered the plates, her voice became bitter.

"I feel rotten pet, rotten, rotten..." She paused to light up a long cigarette, and the fumes spread a form of sickness over the table. Her face appeared older, exhausted, as she smiled at the young woman who had come to help her from the kitchen. Suddenly she began to cough in great hacking bursts and turned away from the man, her shoulders hunched over like a bird, as he stood to help. The younger woman from the kitchen put her arm around her and led her away.

"It sometimes has me pet, it sometimes has me." she gasped.

"Talk about making the tourists feel happy.", he whispered under his breath.

They paid their bill and returned to the afternoon air, where the rain had abated, although the sky above them was still dark and the clouds hung low and grey over the sea. The boats were beneath them, bobbing black shapes far over the water, and by the headland children were climbing like crabs over the ochre coloured rocks; couples walked in pairs alongside the beaten track, and away from them the church and the graveyard stood careless and alone.

They stayed some time there gazing at the texture of ecclesiastical and industrial, melting away into the squat headlands of this Northumbrian coast she had come to love. This coast, his home once here, with its fortresses, castles and ruined churches, measured the distance between mine workings and dock yards, and reflected battles old and new all along the countenance of its forbidding waters and rock strewn beach heads, heavy as if still lying in wait for invaders or class enemies to come out of the mist and dark clouds above.

The man bent over the woman, and with a sort of humorous deprecating gesture kissed her lightly on the cheek. She looked at him for a moment, trying hard not to be shrewd, and cast her eyes down at the rocks and water beneath them. She gathered his hand in hers and rubbed it where his lips had been. Why do we always have to make more of time than time itself will allow us she thought; not just let the years pass and leave them to themselves, and ourselves to ourselves without constructing a set of illusions that always seem to use us.

"No one wants to be isolated love." she quietly rubbed his hand.

He held her with both arms as if impatient to hear more, his collar turned up against the wind and head bent towards her, but her voice trailed away. Looking at him with his longish hair and fixed eyes, she again felt hopeless whenever he allowed her near to speak on his terms. What was bothering him she never really knew, and although her mouth pursed, what she was going to say was diminished down some obscure path, lost within the sound of wind and waves breaking on the rocks.

They walked back to the car, passed the cottages with their gardens and lobster pots on the sheds, passed the old pit where ponies still grazed on the open land and where the new mine, all modern and clean gave way to the modern estate; where finally out of sight of the interminable sea she laid a hand gently on his arm and gave way to the nothingness she felt within her.

" Can't we just learn to exist with each other and not ask too much?"

Her eyes brimmed with tears. Almost like before, the thought of that word rested unspoken between the two of them. Before what? There was only now and she grew angry. It was hopeless.

The rain came back, riding on the wind to strike needles into their faces and make them bend their heads before it like some faraway icon. When they had turned the corner into the culvert he brought the cigarettes out of his pocket, and pressed them into a hand gone cold with wind and solitude.

She didn't care. Where did anybody fit? They were talking about class and about history when they came away from themselves, and the car turned its paces and fashioned some sort of path out of the village, back along the old country roads to their place by the sea.

THE MAN WHO DANCED

The river that Saturday was shot with purple as darkness surrounded the ship. Soon the arc lights were cutting the ropes and spangling the water, and the city lay stilled across from us waiting for the festivities.

And we sat waiting to move to the quays. Cartagena, on our way down from the Windward to the Caribbean basin: Latin America on a Saturday night. Music on the streets, women in bars, and ourselves sullen with injustice stuck in the heat of the river, nothing to do but turn, turn, turn, and wait for Sunday.

Paddy Fagan cut the air of the galley with his bread knife and set out the last of the rolls for the Sabbath. He sat, a stocky figure on his stool and drank from a can of Tennants. The sweat poured out of him. Everyone on the alley called him Barney. He had problems with the heat and worked part of his shift at night away from the swirling humidity and dynamite sunshine of the days. He also acted as a repository of knowledge, or as some would say, a ship's lawyer.

"Barney," I said, "I had a letter in Saint Lucia"

"That's good mate, that's good." He saw my face.

"Even when it ain't good?"

"More so then. Better than going home unknowing."

He dragged an arm across his forehead. I told him then about my Auntie Cissie. She'd looked after him many a time. Took him in when there had always been one too many in Northumberland street. He always used to call her Sis with a great pride, as if it allowed him an entrance to that bigger world. Then she moved across the city. I did not tell him everything. It made me feel like crying, the sight of his face. He came over and shook hands as if he understood.

He was known as a fighter all around our part of the city, and like most fighters he used to sweat a lot. You could see him change his tee shirt twice, sometimes three times a shift, and an hour later it would be run through with fingermarks and perspiration. His gingham checks would be no better, stuck close to him like a wet trencher. He'd wear galley boots with steel toe caps, and he wore those for scrapping when the sailors called up "crap" from below. Now he rolled a smoke and looked out over the rails to the velvet night.

"She was a good woman mate, a kind woman. She looked after me when ....." he was musing, blowing smoke over the side and watching it hang on the water, as if he could see things passing him by.

Away over, the fortress and colonnades are lit by the first fireworks of the night. It was the same at Portobello on a different trip. Watching the empty yellow beach grow dark, and the turquoise creep up off the sea and make its way to the scrubland and the shacks on the hills. The sounds of the cantina and the first shouts coming across the water. The robbers of the West Indies, Drake and Morgan used this river to sack the Spanish Main, but we only wanted the women and the drinking and the dancing that went before them like snakes.

Knowing little of Cartagena we wait for her dusty quaysides and perfumed women, as we waited on the Amazon and the Magdalena. Smoking for protection as we passed the ruined opera house and dilapidated rubber plantations, glorious in the foliage that led to yellow fever and snake bite and animals coming to drink by the stilted houses of the river. Liverpool lives in the Caribbean Basin as it does in the great cities of the Americas. Its citizens at home with the clapping and stamping and singing. And share the same deep unease with the waiting. Time on the anchor is time on the nail. Every bell tells you how much is passing and how much you do not need to be told.

Then crash, the first shouts came up from the customs house. It was party time in our own cantina. The sounds of feet and breaking glass in quick movement. The clump of wood against the bulwarks. The shouts and then more crashing. Hell was a party on your own ship, nowhere to go and no sound of engines to console you. Men who were mad for the women but who had lost something with them dangled their souls on shoestrings, and with the same unknowingness lashed out in the eerie silence of their own company, no matter how shot through it was with song.

"Aw Fuck Off"

Paddy heard the crashes and came running up from the galley. He ran the deck with the excitement coming with a rush from his spine. Abreast of him the ship turned slowly around the pale city, with its stuccoed walls and colonial finery stronger against the light than the flickering yellow fingers of electricity which hardly reached the adobe avenues of the poor with their trumpets and drums.

As Drake and Morgan did not see them, nor did Paddy see the dome of the Town Hall where the soldiers changed places with the Mayor, nor the Cathedral with its brocade of gold and dust where the bourgeoisie prayed and the poor danced, like poor the world over on Saturday night.

The feud was in progress the way it always would be on the anchor, and after the beer and rum and whisky. One of those nights when things go missing. One minute sat listening to a piece of a song, bolting down the cans; then the bottles come out and the light dies a little and the laughs come deeper and the singing longer, with sharp drink, phased intakes of breath and rattling lungs gasping for air amongst the smoke, and the beating in time with the feet and spoons against glasses and hands, and then whoosh it all goes up. No different to a thousand nights when a man holds a grudge.

"Hey Big Feller, when was the last time?"

"I'm nobody's child." They were going country now, the rolling faces of the deck crowd.

Someone crooked a little finger in the air and held it as if dangling a piece of string. This party would never reach "Barefoot Days", the swansong of the Liverpool stokers.

And Hammo MacImmy exploded. The son of a Wee Free and a family of seven from Stornoway. Six foot three and sixteen stone and if that wasn't enough there was more. The bastards had been laughing at him since that time in Grenada. They'd been at it again since the deck crowd were knocked off mid afternoon.

He hated this fucken Liverpool ship. It was in his hands

that cracked against my face, and in all of those yellow and black pictures that swam before me. In all of the shouts of "Ya bas", "Ya bastars" and the falling and the spinning galley boy who looked stupid at his arm; in the chair that took away the deck from the Ordinary Seaman. And in all the spinning room where womanless Hammo was roaring at its centre, and others were falling or running before him. It did not matter that no-one had women. This was a historical hurt.

Paddy burst through the door and butted him. The giant, the begrudger MacImmy. And kicked him with those boots he held for the sailors that bawled out crap. That bastard had been crying all trip.

"Come ye to the fucken deck" MacImmy bawled and lumbered out from the wrecked room like a hippo, his great back, hunched, almost humped around the shoulders. Paddy only felt the anger, felt the blood boil in the velvet roaring night, saw the fight, the fight the way it always would be on nights like these that always seemed to go missing on the point of justice.

"Come ye," the beast had turned and was motioning with its arm. Paddy stood back and hit him again and was bundled out to the deck by sailors, the seraphim of every port.

"Watch yeh fucken self Barney"

I heard them go and looked sideways at the smashed dresser the customs used, and the broken chair. The table was upside down. I tried to set it upright. It fell over. Two of the legs wouldn't hold. I tried to fix them as best I could. The table stood a moment then sank to the floor as though released.

The wrapper rug was wet with beer and patches of blood, the galley boy had been sick by the sink. It looked a mess. There was still some rum in the bottle. I drank it down to steady myself. I found a cigarette and lit it. My mouth hurt and the eye was coming up. I looked out to the lights of the quayside. It was a nice night. You could hear singing coming across the water from the dark streets that backed onto the docks. They were having a good time down there, fighting and dying and forgetting. I went up on deck and stood by the cook who was holding an axe.

Around him were the shadows of the purple night. The silent crowd wedged between winches and hatch covers ropes and cargo nets; fugitives of their own strewn decks in wanting to not alert master nor mate nor engineering official of the merchant marine. Like the dockside of the city across the water and the poor, riotous as lost souls, this was their show.

Barney was circling around. He'd tucked his blue checks into his boots and looked like a little dancer. Fighting off his left, he'd bob forward then feint and jump in with his head. When he came inside he'd manage two or three quick butts, then dance away like the Golden Vision who graced Goodison Park in those days. It was great. Like having our own Fighting Harada. Then Hammo caught him with a hook and there was a clump like the sound of an axe on damp wood, and the crowd shuddered, like when Emile Griffiths was chopping away at poor Benny Parret in New York.

And this silent crowd wanted to scream and roar as they swilled beer. They had forgotten the chipping and the scraping, the endless watches, the loading cargo down the sweat filled hold. They were on the Caribbean coast of the Gulf of Mexico. They knew things about fighting down here; cockpits laced with blood and sweat and all the wild inarticulate roar that accompanies it. Ask anyone who has been at the stadium in Liverpool with the house full and the lights down, or the Bear Pit of any waterfront city. So the crowd stood quiet, holding themselves in amongst the shadows of the deck as the glistening water lapped slowly against the sides, and the fighters made their moves.

His body arched like a trigger every time Barney went forward. He would circle left dragging the big fellow around to the right, and then jump in, flashing his head and his fists following forward like a bronco. Catching his breath he'd try to start hooking off his back foot, and that was when the dark mass moved forward to find its range and blam! The haymaker would start winging.

One of them landed and Paddy went down. MacImmey

stomped him. The cook fingered the axe, but Barney managed to roll into the runnels, and the giant was too drunk to get his feet into his ribs or properly put his lights out.

Paddy got up and the bludgeon stamped forward again, a face of wild concentration scarred with drink. The air reeked of the stuff. But Paddy danced and got one back and opened up his eye. The crew blew out in silent song. They landed that one. There was no tomorrow now. Christ knows who they were punching, but the night rocked with silent rage and hatred.

The trick with Barney, something that he'd learned from his old man and from Johnny Caldwell, was the lightning feet. Use your fists if you had time, but the hooves would bring you position, and if you were small and the world was full of giants, time was everything. There was never enough of it. His old man, one of the hard men of Northumberland street, years in the stokehole, a sharp dresser down the town when he came home and who, like many before him, realised the value of the commodity called love, the old man had taught him that.

Dance, jump, fight and fuck. Barney getting his wind back ripped into Hammo like a whirlwind through the warm Cartagenan night. Proud in the same way the cockpits bred their fighters down here and all along the Mexican borders to this hurricane of a town.

The head and the feet were flying now. All in time the wheeling dance and the jumping galley boots. When Hammo went down, it was a stumbling in the yellow mound of manila that spewed its tentacles across the deck and wrapped like seaweed around his ankles. Drink had not helped. You could see the water shining and luminous beyond him through the railings.

He wasn't going to make it as he slid towards the runnels, hair dragging across the deck. Paddy was at him like a terrier, and the boots were going a mile a minute under the moon. Then like the water through the guards, the great forearms rose in the air in a mixture of piety and mercy and bedraggled with rope, like some huge cargo coming in off the dock. The sailors emerged from the shadows to pull away the still kicking Barney, and the cook put down the axe and went looking for a drink.

The next morning Paddy was as clean and dry as anyone had ever seen him. His hair was washed and tho' his face had great bruises and swelling around the eyes, he had managed to shave, and his cotton shirt was gleaming and his trousers, pressed blue and white, were tucked into his boots as if he knew it made him look the part.

He was smoking a cigarette and leaning out of the galley door and looking over to the white outlines of the port. This same port with its music and song where he would contract gonorrhoea, and spend his days homeward dreaming sullen penicillin dreams that would make his mouth turn to ashes and his bunk a mangled heap of perspiration. But now all the fresh still light of the morning was upon him.

Behind him in the gradual heat of the galley, the old cook fumbled and moaned. That Paddy had turned to was enough. No fighter was expected to work the next day. Hammo remained below for three more in the darkness of his cabin.

Around us, the sailors were lifting anchor and moving us in the sunlight towards the white shining city, with its bells ringing for Sunday and the smell of coffee and cologne on the quaysides and the streets with their music and dust, from which every shack, every tenement, every Avenue and shout filled bar sang Hello. And some sang longer than others.

We came back to Liverpool ten days later, and all the way up the Atlantic it blew and it blew on grey swollen waves beyond the green outcroppings of the Azores.

It was still whipping the river when we came alongside in the Huskisson Dock and stepped through the ropes, and we went up past the gates to see my Auntie who was propped up in bed on Fonthill road. She had posted few letters to the shipping companies in her time. They were generally messages of disaster from our street and from those around us. And like some great historic memory she had always hated the wind, when sails and spars had filled the quaysides and each dock was a small walled town.

I can remember her years ago in our house, sitting all night with my old lady when it started to blow. Now she was dying she said, "Isn't it beautiful son." And struggling up with her arm crooked on the pillow, she'd cock her head slightly to the sound in the chimneys.

"Listen to God's whisper" she would say.

When Barney came in her face lit up as though she was witness to some great and wondrous event. She leant forward and put her arms around him, her sparrow shoulders rocking gently through the nightdress. When he let her lie back, her eyes still shone with the same look of enchantment.

"My one and only son" she murmured, as if settling to herself the weight of the historical debt amongst her smoothed pillows, while those around her did not know where to look or coughed into their hands. Only Paddy had not taken his eyes off her, issued as we were off the streets of our own city, and our lives bound up with Ireland and Chicago and New York.

She died just before we sailed again, and tho' I couldn't make the funeral, Paddy came up with me for the last time and a few pints and to shake hands with the Uncles. I found out later that he had been up every day to see her. Sweat clung to him even in the October air, and he carried a spare shirt in a paper bag the way I heard his old man used to when he was down the town.

As we came up the brow you could see the black mass of the city and the water below us and the railway lines under the moon and our place on the river where the Harrison boats docked. The shirt was for later, the wind blew around us like a dancer, for the clubs and for the women, before we went back again to sit at anchor in the hurricane ports and to wait for the letters, biographies of the poor who had written our history.

HEARING THE WHISTLE

They came up around the coast to Liverpool. Liverpool in the Autumn, how many stories there were to be told about that town. 1968 Liverpool October, black and red; a decanted population despatched to hills and vales that surround the city, and only back together in coloured buses for the match. The smoke across the sea of faces that roar at each other around the field; stanchions that rise out of this bulging heaving sea that curses and bellows and sways and roars and is transformed in the bathe of floodlights. A shining cauldron as the smoke rises blue against the black air beyond the lights. Changed, those thousands from the docks or warehouses, shops and factories, boots and donkey jackets and fag-lipped, hair shining with the brief after-work wash, waiting on Sundays for best suits or sharp-jacketed from the car-works, take brief sauntering walks with papers to the alehouse to read all about it.

On Saturdays, the city at evening, the smell of the hamburger boards downtown. A painting in a cafe selling chips of a Palm boat from West Africa unloading cargo in the sun of the south docks, behind it the great brown-stone cathedral. Trees, a blue sky over the city and dockers and painters and platers and scrapers, millions of them down in history working their patterns into this town's culture. Changed was Jackie, changed with all this; his hopes and fears against the background of fire and the sea, a great place for the dramatics of life. Looking at the picture in his memory, a time far gone of steaming tramp ships and picture postcards of the Harrison boats riding at anchor off East Africa. The roll of the smoke, the sweep of the sun, the memories of entered harbours, what sort of talk was this?

Some memory of what he was supposed to be as the ship came up the river with the weeping sky scratched red over Liverpool Bay, and Jackie washed plates and dusted down alleyways as if his hands were no longer part of him. What was it, the glove dusted magician, the quicksilver glass, the broken jar; standing in line on Winter mornings, shadows rising from the water like dreams.

What talk was this as they approached the locks and voices sang out on the far wall. The beckoners to the dirty city. The ship was well known. The shouting landing crew, all part of the intimacy that a short voyage brings, unlike the great shadows when the ship is away months and everyone looks on the return like an overture. The short trips carve their own patience in faces on the rail. The seamen looking. A city returning their gaze.

Liverpool air. The fire took him from Liverpool air, where the blood has run from many a pinched chest and ruined lung, and tossed him into nights full of stars, and canvas bivouacs hoisted above hatch-tops in glistening nights through the Caribbean. And back to the same old smells, the tanneries, the molasses, the grain and the falling rain spattering mud on the dockside and running down the green warehouse doors. Songs coming up from the radio.

The crowd from below littering every horizon from the Pacific to the Scandinavian sea. The young and slim to those who reside quietly, faded overalls and clean tee-shirt over the paunch. Home, to all night clubs where he had gone before the sea was ever dreamt of, and lay there barbiturate crazed while the women danced. And what balls, tells the cook he used to drink wine down in Tarleton Street until he got sick of it and knocked it on the head. And they got sick of him. The smart-arses they all are at sixteen, with a first trip to come. And what had he come away from? Fairgrounds on the brick-fields, lights in the sky, cartwheels spinning in the dark.

Liverpool, land of fantasy. The western city and the Indies. Grenada, where Eddy had his vision in snatches of song and shaking heads. Where was he now with his hair sweeping down and his arms flung out. The Saint who told him after that last fight to go outside of himself if he wanted to be anyone. And in Spain, where he ignored Jack Kavanagh's talk of prayers, and instead sat on the quaysides with ships and old stories and drink instead of the church. Always the drink to warm them. Benny, the old fireman, Keogh the storekeeper.

Voices and memories of the city sinking away into the dark. When he did break away, drunk outside the dockside parish, eyes would drug over and shoulders sag to the present, as if he were tired of riding the nights, the books, the endless tales.

He opened his eyes and saw again the river. The green vales beyond gave only a background to the docks and the warehouses and mills, where the real city wept and stormed. Between them, the shadows rising off the water, you could see the five faces of the half-tide clock like a statue to the working class, and a watery sun now falling behind Cunard. The white buildings of the landing stage came rising out of the water, as great in their own day as New York. And let no-one tell you the dockers did not know the great poem that was America; their's was the experience of all the dynasties of the waterside.

Before them, catering superintendents waited anxiously; half tide lock gate-men with bicycle clips around their trousers, customs officials, custom crews, deck superintendents, shore gangs, hangers on, engine room, "personnel", shift watchmen ten hours early. All these are shouting and trying to jump aboard as the ship comes through the great churning troughs, the great blackened wood of the inner gates. All with a separate corner to protect, and up above on the bridge of burnished wood and brass, a tut tut tut over whisky. The state of the practice in this queen of overtime ports. Never a night when there is not a docking gang to be raincoat-folded in Winter twilight, the sweet smells of their tobacco filling the bus home after football.

He wasn't thinking this. Couldn't take in the whole breadth of existence which unravelled his days and nights. The nod of a head or the shape of a word, whole decades in the making. The mock laughter amidst the quicksilver glass, the broken jar, the crowds on Lime Street or down that same landing stage. Stood in line while the big ships took on waiters and the favourites stood to one side like prize cattle, smoothed hair and golden ringed against the grey Liverpool river. Cunard Yanks.

And stealing wasn't the all: nor ducking and weaving and

bringing home from broken crates, or taking the corners once in a while. There was more, much more, and years have been put aside to show others there is a wider picture, a bigger story. The docks were full of stories and yet like the sea strangely cast within themselves.

At uncle Billy's death, John Smythe comes up. "Listen son." The old hands fumbling with cigarette paper, tobacco strands falling out onto the pavement. He has taken a drink. Clouds are moving quickly across the sky.

"I've been an anarchist, in the Labour Party, a communist, and do you know what?" The head bent to see where half his cigarette had disappeared. The pressed clothes of retirement flapping around him. The eyes peering up at you. Out from under his daughter's feet. "It's like Saint Augustine said, We don't know where we're coming from and we don't know where we're going." God bless, son.

And death had come to the auntie by this time in 1968. The source of the fire in his early life when, drunk and maudlin, she had burned the house and had the family traipsing across the city, mattress on the wagon, middle of the night, clear sky with stars shining. Liverpool, the pearl in all our souls.

Drunken, our auntie since taking up with the ship's engineer. Shame of lovers calling at her home. The old scores. Arguments with green-coated biddies who wore stout shoes. The cries of lust rattling the windows. The shocked street. Pillars of the Catholic church. The old dead granny who would never have allowed such a thing. And the church her art silk stockings had first danced around fades like an old rose as this Italian looking lady, Liverpool dark, swallows more of the whisky until she sings with it in hoarse croaking mountains of tears. Another drenched soul of Ireland.

Lady gone wrong, who made all in the war and was blown up in the peace when her laughing lovely legs started to take in weather and pour the bottle. Time gone wrong for children. Her only child stillborn. The killer of uncle Billy. And now she walks the Liverpool streets until she arrives alone by the house. The childless February street of severed branches between the pavement and the stars. All gone wrong. Their branches, like herself, alone beneath the moon.

The house, the only possession left from when times were high, and everyone wanted to dance. Great names and she was one. Trips to Italy and to Spain. There was a bottle upstairs. She went to her room, passed the sleeping family on the first floor. A room in this, her house, where she should have had a palace. She strews paper and matches like confetti and watches them fall, and lights them with easy abandon on her knees, the way lust was often wrung from her like a dishcloth. A dancer's palace, to rest, to sleep within.

Standing before the flames, rubbing sleep from young eyes, the mother weeping. Without home, what does it mean? What does it mean for seamen? Liverpool humour that covers the carpet of tragedy, Liverpool fantasy.

They were coming alongside in the Queen's dock. Jackie was losing his grip. The sound in the alleyways was raging with boots, his poor dead auntie and uncle Billy, as dockers and seamen, platers and wipers, screechers and hooters, crane men and tugboat men, catering crews come marauding aboard. Family mafias, street dynasties, company hucksters all singing their own song.

The door was flung open and he pressed cigarettes into the welcoming hands. A home ship in her home dock. A case of beer was on the deck. He passed around the cans. He looked around him, caught the faces who sucked in smoke and slurped at booze, laughing young faces, older ones, browner, more beaten, dignified and the face of an old watchman like his granddad, the heirs of all his generation.

Then his own lonely first-tripper ships; and the silences after the strike. Things once hectic settled to their usual monotony, a few of the deck crowd broke open the bond, someone went mad with an axe, the sun was a blessing and other hopes were murdered. In their place came the tales.

Tales of countless lives beneath the stars. The commands of night weather in great sweeping monologues of time and place. The lights of Montevideo twinkling across the Plate from Buenos Aires. Black nights and the red burn of cigarettes in the pine smelling dark. Celtic and Milan from green fields in Lisbon, Tamla-Motown through the Caribbean.

Times are changing son, derelict shipyards across the river. The tenements and "gardens" of the Inner City; Essex Street and Sussex Street and Warwick Street in the South End, where the carters would come and wait on work. Changing son, going away in the flood that rolls back the second city of the once great Empire, and the poor battled and battered each other for ships as they slept in black rooms and poured down these shire streets to the dock. And Great Homer Street ablaze in the late afternoon; the sun striking yellow and fiery red, and the old great houses bequeathed as slums for those that furnish the port. Great Homer Street and Great Mersey Street, and all those thoroughfares from where money flowed in blood-stained cargoes down the river.

All this inside him. Full of it; yet people the same as ever, unruffled or mad outside. The great chorus of babbling voices, the unfolding of the chorus within: another, drink the ale stops the babbling, another one, then another and the voices are running together, in rhythm, the shine of the cans, the sparkle of the bottles, the sweat starting to run: sweet tobacco.

Was that him sitting there seeing the faces from his bunk, his voice shouting with others until the sounds sang around the cream walls, the brown table and chair; his fingers that turned and opened the beer or poured white rum into little glasses, passed around cigarettes, or was he dreaming? The voices sounded no different, the beer was the same, the trips as sharp .... the smoke clogging up the head. No time to worry than beyond where cargo lies transported in the yard, long or short jags in the void. The great tarpaulin of history when all that is left is to pick up the shillings. The voices were part of him but he was gone. The gone man. Across him the generations flowed like water.

How many mornings had he come down and seen the roof of that dockside station where the trains ran between black walls, built in another time. How many middays on the pool with a quiet pint would he ride back, the afternoon to hang around in, the night to kill. The sea, a circle for all his days. The excitement of going away. The depressions on the tide and river out of Liverpool. Hope in the Caribbean on the way home: the thinking and the reality that never came together except in bits and pieces of broken moments.

Drunk and weaving he said his goodbyes. Strangely formal. They all laughed. "Go on fuck-off." Who did he think he was? "You'll be back next week." Best in its own way, no time for explanations. No bothering with all that "sea gets in your blood" bollocks that bubbles out when anyone talks of leaving.

He walked ashore, mind away in the black October; the wind on the water brushing the lights of the town as it curled around the landing stage, free ... not going back. 1968 Liverpool October. Red and black; colours diminishing like dreams. How many stories were left untold about this town. Stories in Liverpool Winters, stories from New York, stories from Barcelona. The babble in his head, the babble in everyone's head who comes from around here.

There was a shout behind him and he stopped to turn back to the ship, luminous as she lay in the berth. A dark figure came down from the foredeck where no light played, a shadow he recognised as it came close. Joey had taken his bottle with the deck crowd, still tying ropes when others were sat below and Jackie listened to voices.

As he emerged he passed over the books borrowed when they had first come away. And now there wasn't a lot to say.

"Look after yourself kid."

"You too mate, I'll see you."

All their dreams scattered on shipboard visions and what the future might bring, and now silence in the autumn evening. Jackie took the books and put them in his bag. He moved on again through the warehouses towards the Cunard buildings, the brighter lights and behind them, in shadows the mighty birds. His bag held tight as if something might escape.

He was sailing beneath high riding clouds along dark waterside streets. The recurring mish mash of gable walls and alleys in the shadows, the lights of home and stops and starts that haunt anyone who has been away; that illuminates them as only the lighting struck are shown in their strange static dance. Television aerials tacked to crumbling bricks: antennae that creep towards the sky. Bent conductors of the light that comes flickering in every room. Shadowy visions that visit every evening and fly away at dawn. He wanted to be on their wings. To come stealing like mist, like the tides, then disappear. To be around the city he loved or to move. A follower of dreams unconfined to the night.

The voices were running together. The shine was upon him, the extra strokes on the canvas, the gloss on a pint, the cool night air coming off the water, and even as he walked, the sweet thoughts of dreams and possibilities tumbling down; the thudding in his head, the remnants of the drink and the finality of a brick through an abandoned warehouse. Kids ran away as he approached the sound of smashing glass. The black row of desolation between dock wall and the dying mills. The chute overhead from the silo to the quay and the first container boats docking up river.

He stopped to roll a smoke and looked back over the docks. Patches of light shone in pools where the twilight gang continued. Along the road he bought matches at a kiosk run by a cripple who sold newspapers silently in the red evening rush hour but now in the black night mutters of times at sea. No matter any more, Jackie could say the same. The same as a million others from this town. He used to go away.

A HUNGER FOR LOVE

CHARACTERS

Old John a building worker
Maggie Murphy and the very young John
Molly his only remembered lover
A runner
John the young seaman
Narrator
Drunk
A commuters wife?

The action is to take place on and off the stage. At the end
of the play a narrators voice will be heard, it is the last time he
will intrude. There will be no separate number of scenes or acts
in any formal sense. When it is necessary to change some part
of stage equipment, lights should be switched low so as to
lessen the intrusion. In any case, apart from the use of lights
the only props necessary will be a bed, a wall (to lean on) some
ropes scattered about, for the entrance of John the young sailor.
Lastly and probably more important, a hedge that should split
the stage into two halves (both seen directly from a frontal
view). Nothing more should be necessary.

The play opens on a bed that is covered with ragged and
dirty blankets. An old man (old that is, about sixty, building
site old) is in bed, beside him is a large alarm clock. He
rumbles over in bed and one hand reaches out for the clock. He
makes a movement as if to bang down and stop the alarm
bells ringing. There is no sound. He grabs the clock and shakes
it then pulls it up in front of his eyes.

JOHN   (Sitting up in bed) Uh Ugh what's the time, Oh
Jesus. (Suddenly slumps back down, holding his head) Time I
was rising and falling. Oh no, hard on at sixty. It's not on. Why
isn't it? Why even birds rose in the pink dawn when Casement
came ashore. Oh, me head as big as the bloody pier and down
there, down thumpin' an' throbbin' like you do, wantin' to fill
the sheets full of it as if I still could. (Sits up again) The time

sweet Jesus, the time. Pints of it last night. Late, I'm late an no alarm an there's sunshine through the window. Get yer hands off it. Get up, get out. Work. Out of the stinkin' sack. Work, I'll suffer if I don't.

(Enter on to the stage young woman hand in hand with a small child. They ignore the old man, who is up and getting dressed.)

MAGGIE   We goee ta ta's John. We goee tata's wiv Maggie Morphy. What a fine man you'll be. Sure look at the walk on him. I'll bet there's a few miles in them little legs. Oh a fine little walkin' man you are.

JOHN   (Muttering) A fine mornin' mustn't be late. A fine workin' man I am.

MAGGIE   Hand in hand with Maggie Morphy along the beach. Look at the seagulls johnee, hear them crying. Oh the poor lonelys. And the wind blowing our hair an soughing through the dunes.

Can you hear it going whooooh whooo. (They drift off stage. For a brief instant old John lifts up his head to look at them, but then turns away.)

JOHN   Get going, get going. A fine morning it is an all. Fine to be tottering past trees, in the air and the sun to the junction. Bacon cooking, egg on the kiddie's face, better than in its eye. Oh aye it's been in mine the last forty years. Door slams, bye bye darling. Baby wave spoon, gurgles goo goo, byey. I'm here at the junction, me usual junction and where's me lift. Couldn't go without me, wouldn't do (pause) couldn't do. No sign on the open road, neither man, nor lorry nor even a dog to loll in the shadows. They couldn't, they wouldn't.... Better get going (pause) it's not so far, not very far but they'll be waitin' for me.

(The stage lapses into darkness. John walks around the perimeter of the audience. A guitar plays softly. Then a light spotlights the aisle with John walking up it and limping.)

JOHN   Fine to be walkin to work, a decent working man, a mornin walkin in August. Trees, the hay crop, starlings on the tarmac, cows, bullets, crows I can hear your cries. Oh aye, its not hard to guess, between the branches and harsh in the shades.

Thirsty. Me walkin with a stem in me gob to stave off the thought an oh, the thought, the brown holy sweetness of it with young Kavanagh in the pubs an yes Mrs, we'll have a couple off the top shelf of yours. Didn't we take the ferry last year the lad an meself a great crack altogether, us singin' on the rails an the tourists all around us (laughs) what tourists there were on account of the troubles. Ha, holiday time, a great crack, me head boomin' an ragin' an yer mans voice bellowin' out over the water, then it's back to the muck an now me hurry, hurry, hurryin to a trench in Somerset, like a rat goin' back to its hole an it beginnin' to get wet under the armpits an in me cap. Me stem chewed dry, (bends down) ah a pebble, ease the thirst, the achin'. A rock in me gob to run with. Run now John, c'mon. (Tries to run, after a couple of strides ends up limping worse than before, almost hobbling. Goes off the stage but his voice can still be heard saying.)

The pain of it Oh Jesus the pain, but once back there, back there in the old place there was a time.

(The narrater's voice can now be heard coming from the wings. After he has spoken the first line a young figure dressed in running clothes will come gasping up the aisle onto the stage.)

NARRATOR   The green fields, laburnum trees waving and dropping pink petals onto the grass. Masters in cassocks sat on blue folding chairs. Proud housemasters, hard taskmasters. And sports day is just the metal for the glint in their eyes.

RUNNER   (Gasping and moaning) Here we come now, here we come, our ragged numbers ushered in from the lanes. Don't let us down they said (coughs) have I pleased ye father. (There is a sound of cheering)

RUNNER   Old boys are on their feet now. Ye've fine runnin' legs John, now go on will ye gow on. The plod of me pumps on the turf. Wavin' to me. Brother James has hold a stop watch. Me shorts like a rope between me crutch, an vest ablowin' in front. The dolly's pumpin the ground, out on me own now. Tramplin down the daisies, me ears roarin, am I pleasin' ye I'm winnin', I'm winnin' can't you see?

(Crumples to the floor and lies motionless on the stage.)

NARRATOR   Gut and lung strain spewed over yer country, what good did it do. With you spent, and lain breathless on the sweet grass of Saint Micks. Alice an Connie were runnin, their skirts blowin' to you but yer man turned them back. One of yer brothers with his pipe and blanket, red lips an purple cheeks. Away with you an let him be were his words. An himself lookin down an smilin an blottin out the sun, an you thinkin it was the shadow of God 'tween yerself an the sky. Ah ye bloody fool. An him tellin ye that's a fine pair of legs ye got there John, an you sayin bless you brother an the old silver coin spillin down out of his hand ......spillin ....spillin luvely times an cakes an buns an packets o woodies ....ye reward John, ye reward for not lettin them down.

(John comes running and hobbling back up onto the stage.)

JOHN   Cakes an buns an packets of woodies, me reward, ye reward John (without pausing) no no, stop thinkin', let me get..., the job, waiting for me, there's work to be done, work, work, work, a fine pair o legs ye got, no business be walkin', try the trot, a little jigger (runs and then stops abruptly) sweet mother (wipes his sleeve across his forehead) buckets of it under me cap, rolling down me legs, an down there thumpin' an throbbin' an up here thumpin' an throbbin' an me boots, full of it an me head the same way, till I don't know where I'm goin', like a fuckin' machine, runnin' an thumpin an throbbin'. Sick of the sound of it, no no don't think, there's work waitin' (makes sudden attempts to start running again) waitin' for me, me reward; work, in the sunshine, in the cold, the dust, the frost, pink diesel down the maw of me mixer, down the road, waitin', not far, can't be far (Panting). Blessed Jesus keep me runnin', the shimmerin' road, all sunlit pools, through the trees, can't be too... oh Jesus, too long an no time to rest, alleviate me pain, only cows an barns an barns an bullocks an fields criss crossin' the earth, shamblin' by an Molly, Molly, it's all rushin' back to me no no, not here, stop thinkin', keep goin'. Keep goin'. (As John is shambling up and down on the stage, the woman enters and steps into the background. She makes no movements, only her voice is audible above John's laboured breathing.)

MOLLY Keep going John, those forty years and nights you left me, nights, trembling in the stillness, and, dancing wild tangoes down the alleys

JOHN (almost shouting) Molly

MOLLY (not looking at him, nor he at her) Me pale legs John around ye, shivering out our songs to the moon, me head on your shoulder John an' tears an' cryin, when you took the passage alone, you going alone Sean and there's no-one here.

JOHN (his voice hoarse and befuddled). No no not here, not here, too much of that, keep goin, forget it all, forget it ever started, runnin' then waitin' for me, down there, waitin' dig a hole, keep goin' to work an work an work, the only source an curse of the workin, ah shite, can't ye forget it an give yer fucken feet a chance.

(Stops here in the middle of the stage and bends down to take his boots off. Fishes a piece of twine out from his pocket, attaches the boots to it and hangs the boots around his neck. Takes his socks off and rolls them into a ball and puts them into his pocket.)

JOHN (attempting to run again) Better, more room for breathin, me feet swimmin' in the stuff, hampers me runnin', me ole boots bangin' on me chest like lads off to the football. The early days gone now an am shamblin', the shite all over me face an dribblin' from me nose, barefooted an Jesus me boots, the smell of them, holy Mary the smell, wrung out of a million building trenches.

JOHN Concrete and sand and dust all over them. Boots I kicked away me life with. No no not here, forget that, forget all that, keep goin, movin' round the blessed country, runnin', diggin' holes in every county, hands on me shovel, the noise an the rubble, places the people hurry past in fear of the buildin' up an tearin' down. An me only starin' at the walls of the pub an the days goin' by like shadows. Blessed mother, a rest from

118

thinkin', it does no good, get off to work, keep running, an me nights all blurred with thoughts, so lonely, so long ago an Molly, (His head slumps onto his chest) if ye could see the changes.

(He goes off the stage and begins a slow walk around the perimeter of the audience. The sound of a guitar is again heard and slowly gets louder as the lights open on a man leant up against a wall. He's well dressed although his drunkenness make the clothes look as though they hang on him. At the end of the wall is a door. The man is slowly edging towards it, like a boxer at the tenth.)

DRUNK The changes in a workin' man when he leaves his home for a room. The plastic curtains, the chipped enamel of the sink, pissed an spat in, an all the bottles, hundreds of them in a stench of Guinness an milk beneath the bed. Your bloody lonely bed, where they gather cobwebs, yer bed that was once warm an full an creakin' an warm, warm as fire in winter when there was no need to huddle in ragged blankets nor see out the night times of tired singin'.

DRUNK Staggering back, bottles in me pocket to you, Molly (shakes his head in forlorn fashion) no no, you'd gone. Me leaving for the work, for the work to squash me as summer flies, or lights on the dirty pavement with the dawn. The leftovers of the night, alone. An you only an image dribbling over cracked fingers in the light of Sunday morning through the curtains that makes me rise alone, an wash alone an come on home alone from the work that keeps me going. John, what the sweet Christ are yuh doin ?

(He comes back onto the stage after his walk around the audience. Some of them now begin to jeer him, start calling him a bloody fool. The boots are still draped around his neck. There's some blood on his left foot. His limp is noticeably worse and he doesn't speak so clearly now.)

JOHN Just a few steps further or miles, miles gone by. It does not matter, a man like meself, a fine walkin' man, draggin' down the road sunlight in me eyes, movin on and on me fine strong legs an feet that pad the shimmerin' tarmac (loses his step and falls) or stumble into the damp green banks on the side of the way (gets to his feet again).

Ahhh the cool grass against the swelling (looks at his feet) ahh don't bother, the speckled blood between me toes, as dark as the markings on a starlings egg. Don't look at blisters and dirt, a workin man don't ever look. Protect the eyes, blinker the yoke from sun, heat and hardships (jeers from the audience) all the little hardships that as each day goes, turn into mountains. (He stops and pulls his cap down harder over his face.)

Keep going, blinkered, sweat over the road, me face invisible to angry eyes an me juttin chin goes on and on, a shadow passes sometime over it like it does now, an then when I think of sailors on forgotten ships an fog bells crying into the night when we killed the days with drink.

(The lights go down here and John hobbles backwards and forwards across the stage. When they go up again John's shoulder is more severely stooped and the boots hang heavy around his neck where the twine is beginning to cut the flesh. In the background a young man can be seen sitting on a coil of rope, dressed in a work shirt and canvas trousers and smoking a cigarette. Like the other characters, when he speaks he doesn't look at John but at the audience, although there can be no doubt it is the old man he is interested in.

John for his part keeps moving backward and forward across the stage, shoulders stooped and hobbling.)

YOUNG SEAMAN Aye you were a sailor John an dragged and dragged wild ropes over shifting decks an the road also sways an shifts an you rollin with the blow, seven crusts for seamen and a million hurts, but nothing, nothing like stars you gazed at in the China sky. Ahh yer sick of it now but then, young, young an sailing were full of it on the seas and rivers an quaysides and quick taken lovers in back crack houses. Aye you were young John, young and sailing and never for a moment thought old men were dying.

JOHN Aye old men are working but don't think, keep going, shamblin' waiting for me down there, dig a hole, keep going, quick now down there in Somerset, feet on me shovel, head down, don't look up. Donegal breeds workin' men. An a fine walkin' man I am but Jesus sick. Sick of the sight and sound of it, sick of runnin', sick of bein alone but no no, don't think it, get on, get on....... (stops suddenly) music, can hear music, no no, me ears, the flies (Shakes his head) music, real music yes I can feel it. Blowing across me like the wind. (The sound of a radio can be heard beyond the bend.)

(This is the nearest we get to a separate scene. John comes off the stage and the lights go down after he has said his last sentence. The guitar continues to play as it has done in other change overs. The tune if any should be "Damn your eyes". The scenery for this act shows a country bungalow with a hedge around the front garden. It is impossible to see the garden from the stage but we can hear from behind the hedge the sound of a radio playing. The lights go up as John re-enters.)

JOHN   A house, a house there in the sunlight, water, sweet Jesus stumblin on towards it, legs no good no more, need water. (Stops before the hedge) Little songs, sunny mornin's, dear God the wasted times. (He spends some time peering over the hedge then turns back to the audience.) The woman there, lying down, bathin suit oh luvely, O holy Jesus all brown an tanned. (Turns swiftly back to the hedge) Maam Maam maam, dyin of thirst some water maam (reprimanding himself) - Be decent now, pull your cap up, slap your hair - Please maam.

NARRATOR   The woman sits up, she looks sharp, her head slopes back like someone hit. There's fear in her eyes, fear in her skin, her car's in the garage she looks up again.

JOHN   (His head and his neck over the hedge apart from his boots that are lodged against his chest. There is a widening red mark from the twine that attaches them to his neck.) Maam some water. Was runnin maam, work maam down in Somerset, no lift Maam, they left me. Have to run maam down there, dig a hole they're waitin, dig a hole down there. Sick of it, sick of it Maam but some water. Terrible thirsty.

(There is a brief silence then three screams can be heard, each one louder and longer in intensity, as John remains at the hedge.)

JOHN   No maam, no maam please, just some water.

(To hide her screams he puts his hands over his ears.) Strange, the sticky wetness (takes them down and looks) Blood, blood on me fingers, biting me neck, pulled by me boots rubbed by me runnin' an she screams. Blood on me feet blood everywhere an all she can do is scream at me blood an' dirt an' blisters an' now she's runnin' runnin' runnin away, away inside her red bricked house. She's gone John. She's gone.

(Lights go down. Hedge and other parts are whisked away. He stands there, breathless on the stage, not entirely unaware now of the heavy boots he carries around his neck, not knowing quite what to do.

As he stands there and faces the audience, the other characters begin slowly to pass across the stage behind him. The first is Maggie, who walks hand in hand with a small boy.)

MAGGIE   A fine little walkin' man ye are John an there's the wind from the dunes blowin' in yer hair an some fine miles in them little legs.

JOHN   Fine miles ye say, (rubbing his hand across his face) Oh Jesus don't think, but what did she run away for?

MOLLY She's gone John like you'd gone to leave your home for the work an me here alone an you there alone an no more the wild tangoes an' now them waiting on you to dig all the holes in the world.

JOHN   Aye they're waitin' all right for diggers of holes an' shite. For hands on iron shovels to go trundlin' around the country.

RUNNER   Runnin, father ye said keep runnin', the legs on ye like an old horse, am I pleasin' ye, am I pleasin' ye now I'm winnin', winnin' now, out on me own fathers, can ye see me?

JOHN   No-one sees you when the weight of bricks bends ye back or cement dust burns yer eyes an hair, an all that's left of an army of feelin' is when the job's finished an stands there alone, cold an alone, an the men go, flung away like stones.

DRUNK Alone, an' your bloody lonely bed, yer bed that was once warm an full an creakin'. Ah sweet Jesus the changes, the changes in a workin man when he leaves his home for a room, an there's only night times of tired singin' to accompany him home.

YOUNG SEAMAN But once he was young, young an sailing wild an free an little did he think old men were dying, nor would be waitin', huddled in the cold, stayin' close to the huts, not wantin' to go when the siren blows an day begins. And for all the world, day begins.

(After the sailor has spoken there is a brief moment of silence, John is standing with his head bowed, the house is still depicted behind him.)

JOHN (quietly) But she screams when she sees me. What likes have I done except build their houses on scaffolds when it's freezin' or their roads in summer with the asphalt splashed all over ye (raising his voice a little) don't think, don't think they say, keep going, keep workin' but how much is a cup o water? (Shouts). Why no water when its us that dig their ditches with the stuff that's in our boots, an our broken horizons pay for their finery an all we see is our shovels an don't know why our trains were somehow missed an our boats sailed away. (Lowers his voice) It's us, it's us that are left to pay, an remember thinkin', lyin' in me bed an waitin for the whistle of the Cork train an knowin', it wouldn't come, the darkness, an the lights, runnin' in flashes through Finsbury Park across the wall an thinkin' then how much they've taken. How much they've taken.

(He moves across the stage and sits down. He takes the pair of boots from around his neck and places them down by his side.)

JOHN But no more. No further. No more starting nor wonderin' what's wrong, no more cards in me pocket searchin' and livin' a life alone. No, no more comings in the dark to empty houses. No more runnin' no more shovellin' no more workin' for them to scream at ye like you were the worst insect come up from the soil an deny you when ye needin'.

(The lights are dimmed here. The only change in scenery is that the hedge has been taken away. In the background is still the frontal view of the house, however by the introduction of a small table and telephone upon the stage, it will give the impression of the interior of the house.

The lights open. A woman appears on the stage. She's dressed in a yellow bathrobe thrown lightly over her bikini. Her skin is tanned and her hair short and well cut. There is a large ring on the finger of her left hand. A cigarette is in her hand as she paces up and down the stage but she hardly takes more than a cursory puff of it. John is sat at the front of the stage slightly to her right. From time to time the woman stands and looks at him, she looks most worried then and indecisive, and draws in and exhales in great streams of smoke from her cigarette. Finally she runs to the table and picks up the phone.)

A COMMUTERS WIFE   Police please, yes, police (exasperated air) I know I'm not dialling but .... (a moments silence.) Hello, police? Oh officer so glad, a man outside constable in terrible state. Hanging himself. Yes sergeant, a rope, everything. Saw him at the hedge. Cap across his eyes. Yes, a blindfold, oh terrible (without raising her voice) at wits end officer. Please hurry, a car (pause) right away, oh thank you. Don't know what we'd do without .... No officer I won't leave. (Puts down phone)

(She continues to walk the floor, only broken by stops to gaze at John or to light a fresh cigarette.)

JOHN   The crucified fucken navvie. (His shoulders imperceptibly begin to sway) out of his shift, out of his time, let loose to go wanderin and think of things best forgotten.

JOHN   But no more ye hear me. (He gets to his feet and picking up the boots by the twine twists them above him in the sunlight, like a bolero. He is in the garden now and lashes them at the house. They sail broken through the air. - Woman opposite him on stage.)

JOHN   No more, forgotten lines, broken dreams, boots thrown away like old fruit into your rubbish and you sittin there in yer fine houses, scattering yer scorn like seeds. No fucken more.

There is the sound of breaking glass. The woman puts her hands to her face and recoils back. She is standing by the telephone like it was a haven, a relief, a safe passage from the storm around her. She stands as if slapped, a little girl.

NARRATOR   An it's for every man to tell his story but how little time, how little time they give for the memory. We read a stanza from the "Great Hunger" and invoke the poet, Patrick Kavanagh as we look across at John. Everyone gone John.
"The pull is on the traces, it is March, and a cold old black wind is blowing from Dundalk."

FADES.
(A police siren can be heard wailing and coming closer.)

EPILOGUE

An old man who had gone away said to me across the bar, "If you want to learn what Scotland Road was like before they stripped this city, then walk down to the harbour in Naples". The Spagganopoli, the dividing line of the old city, heaves and throbs like Paddy's market after the war. There is scaffolding everywhere supporting the alleyways of Gregoria de Armenia. Tenements filter the sun. Card tables support men in white vests, whistling and shouting, clapping, rubbing their bellies. Heaps of fruit are piled on wooden barrows. A funeral cortege emerges from a darkened court. Sweating black horses pull a silver embossed coffin on a carriage heaped with flowers. Behind them five polished black cars draw sombre steps. The traffic shrills and blasts around them. Urban police blow on their whistles, shout at children jumping across ropes, strung across alleyways like the districts themselves, Forcella, San Lorenzo, San Guiseppe and Pendino in this maze of streets behind the great port, as great as he had once known Liverpool.

Tenants fight with the authorities to clear the rubbish, to purify the water, to end the protection of assassins and thugs. Workshops hum with machines. Ten year olds roar down alleyways on red Yamahas, balancing white boxes behind them. Off the Plaza Gerolomoni votive offerings and lighted lamps burn in hollows of the black perspiring walls. Splashes of sunlight come like sudden paintings in the dark. Saint Anthony's convent beseeches, stretching above the street, its yellow stonework stung with fading graffiti, "Grazie a Diego", "Grazie a Napoli". Maradonna long gone in a cloud of drugs but the memories remain, "You did not desert the city, the city deserted you". His picture above you, riding like a sail between the rooftops with the washing hanging from the sky, "Napoli non e Italia". Liverpool is not England.

Everywhere you look, statues of Saint Gennaro: patron of this southern city, yellow statues the size of your finger or as big as a house, crowding the overflowing pavements. Incense burns in rooms with motorbikes. Canaries sing in cages. The tortured face of Saint Peter stares at your ankles, painted upside down across a tenement wall. To deny him thrice !!!!!. Women carry marionettes to the hospital of dolls. Contorted faces peep at you from shopping bags, at cigarette sellers, flower sellers, bicycle and bird sellers, men asleep beside posters of angels with flutes, Courtyards like Chagall's portray San Gennaro's illuminated face bleeding for the city while those from the North say, "We could live like the Swiss if it was not for them".In Britain it is those from the south who voice similar sentiments.

Napoli,the city of the boxer,the drinker,the aggressor,the laughter like Liverpool's,like New York's,a state of mind more than acting the part,with one face for itself and another to the world,to a wider Italy,England or America that is past caring whether it sinks or falls and even less for the politicians who have failed to define its post war world with what one called, " A hell disguised as paradise,a paradise disguised as hell."

Two steps across the Piazza Gugliemo Pepe the sun gleans the water.From the bars and wooden tables of the harbour you can see the ferries for Ischia, Sorrento and Capri,cargo boats for Africa and the Americas,the fishing fleet at the end of oily jetties.Washing hangs on drainpipes.Containers are lifted direct from ship to wagon.The carriages buckle like loaded horses in the sunlight.Dockers come off ships and an half an hour later,shining and showered,load up on soup and wine and chops.Music and shouting comes from the portworkers hall adorned with it's communist posters.

The song floats over clusters of purple flowers growing next to the silos.Red bourganvillea trails down a chandler's wall.A freight engine makes the line in the late afternoon light.The brown cars move over the shale.Walking alongside,the easy saunter of a railwayman,carrying the gloves and flags,like one of Kerouac's linemen on the run from California to New York.You have a beer outside the Italia - Atlantic bar and listen to the distant roar of the city like you used to do in Liverpool.

Walking back,you see little knots of people holding candles outside the convent Fraternita di San Maria Del Carmine.Scaffolding that supported a tenement has collapsed in the Forcella.Mothers pray in the shadows.The heavy dialect murmurs across the evening plaza.There are five deaths and thirty injured.The poor,short changed again,use their prayers in solace."Anche i ricci fiangono", is written across the wall.Translated it reads,"even the rich must cry" but there was not much evidence of that.

Then why does it make you dance? Maybe because of the people and their streets, the city itself against the water, against the world.Like anyone in the presence of death, and always alive to its own story,it sucks you in and chews you like the chops and pasta and salad they all eat in the portside cafe's.Maybe our true home is what others see in us.As Borges wrote, "if you want to describe New York then picture Buenos Aires". With the marine light billowing like muslin across the streets and the first lozenges of yellow appearing in the tenement windows you knew the old seaman had said a mouthful.

He carried within him the dividing lines of place and learning, class and love for his own beautiful city.His city: his cathedrals in the sunlight as great as Naples or New York. Liverpool as she is sung on a cold April night wind on all the way stations from Sandhills to Seaforth and across the docks that cradle the river beneath the same European moon.